After August

After
August

William R. Burkett, Jr.

**The New
Atlantian Library**

The New Atlantian Library
is an imprint of
ABSOLUTELY AMAZING eBOOKS

Published by Whiz Bang LLC, 926 Truman Avenue, Key West, Florida 33040, USA

For information contact
Publisher@AbsolutelyAmazingEbooks.com

ISBN-13: 978-0692534175 (New Atlantian Library, The)
ISBN-10:0692534172

For Shirrel Rhoades, who believed
in this novel when others didn't ...

After August

Chapter One

October 14, 1993
Dear daughter,

It's another hot muggy day at the Beaches as I finally take pen in hand. If you ever read this I will be dead and probably buried. That Jacksonville lawyer who was a public defender when he was a kid just out of law school has promised to take care of all the arrangements. He's a bigshot private attorney now, with his own firm, but he's all right in my book. He didn't let them convict me of first-degree murder in the end, though I didn't give him much help. This was way back when, as we always used to say way back when, and Florida was not squeamish about the death penalty. The Jacksonville State's Attorney acted like he personally wanted me dead when I wouldn't tell him anything he wanted to know. Still thirty years in Raiford is a long time out of a life for what I did.

They paroled me back to the Beaches finally a couple years ago, but everything is so changed here. The whole world is changed I guess. The hardest thing to get used to after I got out was what had happened to the value of money. Before I went away, the minimum wage was supposed to be a dollar an hour. You couldn't even get paid that a lot of places. No waitress at a restaurant I cooked at ever made a dollar an hour, that's for sure, let alone busboys.

Gasoline was twenty-one cents for premium leaded. The only unleaded gas back then was Amoco; people with motor scooters and outboard motors went to the Amoco station to fill up. You probably don't remember any of this.

There was nobody left on the Beaches who

remembered me or had even heard of me. Dawson's Famous Seafood Restaurant had been turned into a Mexican place, phony stucco and all. The big screen dining porches that used to catch the ocean breeze were bricked in and plastered over, for God's sake. Dawson had been dead over ten years when they let me out, bust a blood vessel arguing with a fish seller in Mayport over price.

What had been the best seafood restaurant on the north coast of Florida from Prohibition to the Reagan Administration, a destination stop for rich people riding the Silver Meteor between New York City and Miami, was just gone. I didn't find a single person who remembered the legends of Arab princes hiring taxis at the train station in Jacksonville to come to Dawson's, handing out ruby baubles to waitresses they liked. It was actually a Lebanese prizefight promoter, and an emerald pinky ring. She found it on the bedside table at Bennett's Motel after he left early to catch that morning's Meteor to Miami. Whether it was a tip or forgetfulness, she sold that ring for enough to make a down payment on a chicken farm back home in North Carolina and we never saw her again. Maybe her family still runs it.

There used to be a pedestrian walkway on an arch over Beach Boulevard where it dead-ends at the beach. Teenage boys used to stand up there and look down into cars driving out onto the beach to check out the girls' legs through the windshield, or the entire girl if she was in a convertible. They don't even let cars drive on the World's Finest Beach anymore. I never drove my Chev on the beach anyway because I didn't want to rust out the underside.

More than half of the old one-story tourist traps that used to make up downtown Jacksonville Beach were boarded up or gone, and so was the bandshell. The boardwalk joints were pretty well all boarded-up. There was just an empty lot where the Ferris wheel and merry-go-round and Mighty Mouse roller coaster used to be. Mac's Pool Hall was just another empty building with faded hurricane tape on the windows.

The lifeguard station was still on oceanfront, but the seawall it used sit on was gone, replaced by riprap and trucked-in sand. There was a hellacious hurricane named Dora that knocked it down not long after I went away. There were miniature sand dunes running along most of the oceanfront property now. Beach sand had started building dunes over the riprap and sand that the Corps of Engineers trucked in to stabilize the beachfront.

A couple of those modern name-brand motel chains had built a handful of five- and six-story motels on the beach-front until somebody passed an ordnance to make them stop, so that people who lived back off the beach could still see the ocean and get the breeze. The ones they built looked big and out of place in a one-story town.

The only places besides a couple of motels that were still around and had the same name were the Christian Science reading room across from where the band shell used to be and the first pizza joint that ever opened up on the beaches, way out by the Intracoastal Waterway bridge.

Jacksonville Beach blocked traffic off a lot of First Street, so you can't follow the coast straight north from Beach Boulevard to Atlantic Boulevard anymore. Third Street's the main thoroughfare now. People ride bicycles on First Street, or jog, or skate on those funny Outer Space roller skates they have now. This is grown people doing all this now, not kids. I can't get over dozens of men and women out running or riding their bikes or skating in the dusk. Not to get away from anything, or go toward anything. Just to keep moving, because they think it'll make them live forever. They reminded me exactly of all those cons who pump iron down at the penitentiary for the same reason.

I felt like The Invisible Man in broad daylight. The ocean was the only thing that was exactly like it always had been, and those big pelicans that patrol the surf line like Second World War dive-bombers. Not that anybody I mentioned this to had any idea what a dive-bomber looked like.

Most of the traffic now is those funny little Japanese cars shaped like half-melted bars of soap. Before I went away we hadn't heard about Honda motorbikes, let alone Honda automobiles. About the only cars that I could identify were old and rusted out unless it was somebody's special baby, all waxed and polished and rolled out only on weekends. I did still see Volkswagen bugs, and they still seemed to start every time, like that Woody Allen movie. If I still owned my 1955 V-8 Chev, it would be a collector's item (!)

A lot of people who live at the Beaches work in Jacksonville now. The city has sprawled out almost to the Waterway. Somebody started up some kind of petition to secede the Beaches from Duval County and call them Ocean County. I'm over seventy years old as I write this. I don't know if I still have the right to vote or not, but I signed the petition anyway. Beaches people always were different.

The only useful thing I know how to do is cook. The minimum wage now is more than I used to make working for Dawson as head cook, when I was paid about as good as anybody in the food business. They pay me this new minimum wage for graveyard-shift short-order work at a 24-hour joint out on Atlantic Boulevard where there was nothing but palmetto scrub and cabbage palms when I went away. They were glad to have me, and don't bother me in the kitchen, but I have not been able to put any money by for you. I can just barely rent a room and pay the electric bill for an air conditioner. I need that air conditioner at my age after all those years at Raiford. The bus service has improved on the Beaches, so I don't need to worry about a car anymore, and somebody always needs a cook, even in this world.

All I have to leave you is that one old paid-up life insurance policy from the 1950s, when ten thousand dollars seemed like all the money in the world. My lawyer says there should be some of that left for you after disposing of my remains. That, and a cardboard box that typewriter paper came in, full of these pages that I wrote while I was in prison.

Your mother would have said I should not ask my own daughter to read such a thing. My trial was in all the newspapers and the true crime magazines, and I know she was humiliated about that. I wouldn't ever want her to read about what really happened, but she's where nothing can hurt her now. You're my only living blood kin. It's entirely up to you whether to read what I wrote or get rid of it. Writing it all down was all that kept me going for a long time as the years rolled by.

I started to write this for that lady teacher they brought into the prison back in the 1960s, supposedly to prepare some of us to be better citizens if we ever got out. I had a long time to go, but the warden got me in the class because he liked the seafood meals I prepared with the special supplies he brought in when he hosted bigshots from Tallahassee, so he could brag about having the head cook from Dawson's Famous Seafood Restaurant in his kitchen.

The teacher lady said us cons, especially the ones in for violent crimes, were "conflicted" (I wrote it down) and unable to express our true feelings. The exercise she made us do was to write about things we couldn't talk about.

It reminded me of your schools, when you had to

write, "what I did on my vacation," remember? Remember that St. Petersburg teacher in the third grade who said you shouldn't scare the other children by writing about visiting your mother in the TB sanatorium? People these days don't remember how terrifying tuberculosis was back then. As bad as polio was, almost. Hell these days they don't even remember the polio panics.

So anyway, I started to try to write about what happened to me on the Beaches the way the teacher lady told us to. I got to trying to remember everything exactly right, and I just kept on writing it and changing it and writing it and changing it for a long time. I bet the teacher lady never expected anything like what I finished up with, but I'll never know. She didn't get to see any of it, because in a year or so the Department of Corrections got over worrying whether we were conflicted, or could express our true feelings, and cut the program. I never did know what happened to her. So I just kept writing. I learned how to use the little portable typewriter in the chaplain's office and finally typed the whole thing up, mistakes and all. I never could type very fast, but I had plenty of time...

Chapter Two

We moved to North Florida the summer after the hotel in Saint Petersburg found out about Christine's TB and let me go. I had my state health card and there was nothing wrong with me and they knew it, and Chris had been in the Lake City sanatorium for most of two years, but they let me go anyway.

They said they didn't want their winter guests, rich retirees from the North, finding out the head cook had a wife with TB. The hotel manager was mad as hell that he found out about Chris from a Pinellas County health inspector instead of from me.

I knew that the health inspector had been tipped off by the Tampa cops out of meanness. I had cooked at a particular Italian restaurant in Tampa before I got the hotel job, and the cops figured I was still connected to the crowd that ran *bolita*. It didn't really matter how they found out though, once the hotel management knew Chris had TB.

You almost had to live in those times to realize how scared people were of catching TB. Scientists had started coming up with new drugs every time I looked, but people still were scared of it.

I moved north, and clear across Florida, to a job at an all-night truck stop with a good recommendation from that same Tampa restaurant. Florida is a lot bigger state than some people seem to realize. Before all these expressways and computers, you could drive eight hours on those old two lane truck routes and still be in Florida, but leave trouble behind you.

We took a place on the Beaches to live, and wound up

closer to the TB sanatorium in Lake City where Christine spent most of her time anyway, not too far from where her folks lived in central Florida. The Beaches are on the Atlantic Ocean side, up near the Georgia border, far enough north that their tourist season was the summertime.

After we moved to North Florida, I saw the road crews build a lot of Interstate 10 between Jacksonville and Lake City, driving over to visit Chris at the sanatorium. It was an easier drive than that long run up through Orlando from Saint Pete. That was back when Orlando was nothing but a small pretty town in orange grove country with a big fountain in the middle of the downtown lake. I used to stop to eat at a diner where I could watch the fountain on trips to the sanatorium.

I started leaving Sally with Christine's folks the summer I got fired in St. Pete. She missed her mom and she could go see Christine whenever Christine's parents went. We agreed for her to start school over there. After that I was by myself most of the time. I made it through the first slow winter season at the truck stop only because the owner had some odd jobs outside the kitchen he let me do. Their kitchen wages weren't anything like the hotel's had been, and the sanatorium and those new antibiotics for Chris weren't free.

Dawson called me up out of the blue that next spring and invited me in to talk to him. I was amazed he even knew who I was but he told me he kept his eye on all the bush-league joints six counties around, and people had been talking about my food since I started at the truck stop. It was like being called up to the Cincinnati Reds from the farm system. Most people would say the Yankees but I'm Ohio born and bred.

The Beaches were a summer tourist spot for working people from all over the South, who had to take their vacation when their kids were out of school. After August the official summer tourist season ended and Dawson's cut back on hours and then closed at the end of September, only opening for Thanksgiving Day and maybe some holiday parties. When Dawson's closed after my first summer I did a few more errands for the truck stop owner, nothing to tell IRS about. I had plenty of time to go over and see Christine and Sally then. The unemployment money covered my gas since I had no declared income, and Christine's folks fed me and gave me a place to sleep. When Dawson's reopened the next spring it was almost like I'd been there all my life.

Every Friday night some of the locals who hung around the Beaches bars summer or winter would chip in together on a room at Bennett's Waterfront Motel and play poker all night. Summers I would go over after we closed the restaurant and play. Since I got there late, I usually played until dawn and then walked down the boardwalk and cut over to the Steak Shack for coffee before going home. It got to be my weekend habit pattern.

I liked that first part of the morning with everything fresh. Even flotsam washed up by the night tide had a clean salt smell. The drunks sleeping it off on the boardwalk benches looked comfortable. The little town would be still and empty in the first bright rays of the sun, coming flat-out across the ocean. There would be nothing moving but the big green street sweeper, and the swamper at the Mermaid Bar. The smell of the swamped- out bar when I walked past was weak Lysol and whiskey and stale air- conditioned air. Somehow it was a happy smell to me and I always walked that way to get a whiff of it. After I had my coffee and read the morning *Times-Union* I would walk back to the motel for the Chev and go home and fry some eggs for breakfast.

I had a cypress-shingle garage apartment that year

about six blocks back from the ocean that was pretty reasonable at yearly rates. There was a couple of old automobiles rusting out in each of the garage bays. One had its engine out on a table and the other one's was scattered all over the greasy concrete. The owner didn't want to pay to move them, so she just knocked a few dollars off her original price if you were willing to park under the sun porch overhang. Christine would have hollered about living over a junkyard, but I didn't care.

The Chev was the first new car I ever had, and I always parked it up under the porch to keep the salt air off as much as possible. I parked it so long in the same spot there got to be grooves where the water stood in wet weather.

The place was always sort of eerie-quiet without Chris or Sally them there. The first sun hit right through the rusty porch screens and filled all the rooms with brightness. I would go straight to bed after I ate because it was no use trying to sit up and think about what might have been when the apartment was strange like that. I never had trouble sleeping. I slept like a dead man. I would sleep until Mabel, the cashier at Dawson's, would give me a ring. She just let the phone ring until I would roll over and pick it up and say "Okay, Mabel." I never said anything else to Mabel on the phone; it seemed kind of silly when I would see her in an hour. Mabel understood about me not saying anything, or else just didn't give a damn. If she ever forgot to call, Dawson would always remind her.

Dawson was a hard man to figure out. I gave up trying. He gave me the job even though I told him straight out about Christine. He didn't give a damn what was wrong with my family as long as the state health people had issued me a card. He didn't worry about what made other people tick either. He just wanted his restaurant to open on time, and his customers to be kept happy. If Mabel calling got me to work, and if I was a good enough cook to keep the customers happy, then she could keep on calling me every day until she retired or I died, for all he cared. Then he would have to get another cashier, or another head cook, and then he would. He had a very simple kind of logic. It was a Florida kind of logic that fitted the Beaches very well. What was good for his restaurant was fine, and what wasn't, wasn't even worth thinking about.

The second summer I was there, Dawson started talking about staying open with regular hours all the way until Christmas, because the Blue Dolphin and the Jade said they might. Before now, Labor Day weekend had always been the last big weekend of the season for all three, and they would start laying off waitresses. By October, Dawson's usually was closed until the big Thanksgiving Day football game in the Gator Bowl, when he hoped the Beaches would be one big football party. But this year he was talking about staying open. If he did I would have less time than I had thought this winter to go over and see Christine and Sally.

Corinne was a waitress, one of the new ones who turned up every season all over Florida looking for the big tips. She always had to walk a long mile home from work, or take a taxi if she was too tired, because the bus service was lousy.

I gave her lift home a couple of times the first month she worked there. I liked to hear her talk. She was fresh from deepest Georgia and had a language all her own. I figured she was good for one season before she drifted somewhere else, and that would be the last I ever saw of her. Now, with Dawson talking about trying to stretch out the season, it looked like she might be around the restaurant a while longer. It surprised me how glad I was about that.

Chapter Three

*L*ooking back now, it still seems strange about how it started with Corinne. I was over forty. She had just turned thirty, even if she looked almost like a teenager, still kind of rounded out and baby-fat soft with those big brown eyes and that sleek chestnut hair in a white mesh hairnet. The Florida sun hadn't dried her out yet. And Florida hadn't had time to grind down her Deep South conviction that she always was right in whatever pointless argument the waitresses always were getting into. She just kept right on arguing and never backed down. Most of the older waitresses were like me: they didn't have enough convictions left to break wind with. The younger ones didn't have her machinelike determination.

She was slow on the floor that first summer, but she was a very thorough waitress. Her style of waiting tables shouldn't have worked in a Florida tourist trap, but did. She didn't know how to grovel, or to be elegant. She just found out what people wanted and got it for them like she was happy they had asked. She never missed. Never. When she brought the orders back, they were straight, and they were right. I never had to backtrack on one of hers. I noticed that first about her, I guess. A brand-new waitress who does the job right the first time is hard to find.

Her goddamn small-town uppityness put me off, though. She was certain that no Arabian prince had got off the Coast Line Silver Meteor in Jacksonville and hired Cadillacs to bring his harem to Dawson's to eat because its fame had spread worldwide. She told the other waitresses they were morons if they believed this same fairy tale prince handed out sapphire rings big as marbles to the waitresses that night. The other waitresses were just as sure that it had all happened just that way and might again, any night. I asked Dawson about the Arab once, and he just grinned and said it made a great story, didn't it?

Besides thinking most other women were plain gullible, Corinne was death on men, as men. As cooks or cops or mechanics she allowed that they were all right, if they knew what they were doing in their chosen work. But men as just men, they were nothing. She told everybody that she had married and then dumped two of them in a row, after having a son by each, two different soldiers. One had been stationed near her hometown before D Day, but couldn't keep it in his pants with all the grass widows around the base and got caught at it by her brothers. I figured D-Day might have seemed pretty tame to him after that. The second was a hometown guy she married after V-J day who turned out not to be the same happy boy who had gone off to the Pacific. She kept the kids.

She would tell all and sundry that her Confederate grandmother warned her when men got that soulful look in their eyes, it just meant they had to pee. Some language. She was a tough number, all right. I figured she was raising a pair of pansies, all right. That was before I knew anything at all about her family situation.

Now this was only a dozen years after the war ended, and way before it seemed like every other marriage in America was followed by a divorce. Corinne was the only divorced woman in the place, the only divorced woman that some of us had ever been around.

She looked to me like the kind of ripe big-bodied woman a tough paperback private eye like Mike Hammer would punch in the mouth and then screw. I liked to read all those twenty-five cent Pocket Books back then. I liked Shell Scott even more than Mike Hammer because Shell Scott had a sense of humor.

But Corinne would have had news for Mike Hammer. She told us that when she was a kid her nickname was Jack Dempsey because she beat up every tough boy in her school, and she hadn't forgotten how to punch. She was really something. That broad Georgia drawl was a mile wide and twice as sassy.

Her looks and her being a divorcee made her a kind of a target for local men on the prowl that summer, but only once to a customer. I never knew exactly what she told them in person when they made a play. I knew better than to ask them, the way they kind of wilted when she said whatever she said.

I only saw her actually hit somebody once that summer. It was a weekend, late, and a big insurance company crowd from Jacksonville had been meeting down the road, and reserved the entire sea porch.

This guy she whacked was in a nice suit but had been hitting the liquor pretty heavy, and he made a heavy pass. I was at the order window when it happened. I actually saw him slide his hand up her leg under the hem of her white waitress uniform. I was opening my mouth to yell for Dawson when she calmly snapped her elbow right back into this clown's throat.

He upchucked right in his own lap. Fell over on the floor, coughing and gagging. I thought she'd killed him. She dumped a glass of iced tea on his head and he let out a pretty good howl, so it looked like he would live after all. Dawson was out on the sea porch by then. He got in between Corinne and the customers. Kind of like an umpire holding off a batter who's trying to get a pitcher who beaned him.

The suits from the big insurance company pitched quite an uproar. They claimed Corinne had been leading him on with that honey voice and then assaulted him. This was before 911 and all this modern crap, cops sticking their noses in everything. Restaurants dealt with problems on their own.

When the suits said Corinne had been leading this jerk on, she got ready to whip the bunch of them. I had the busboys out there with me by now to back Dawson's play. On the Beaches, restaurant people stuck up for each other in those days. Dawson just laughed at them, called them sorry excuses for men, and told them to get out. Not before they paid the full tab, though.

I guess right then I should have known how much I liked her. I took my heaviest Solingen blade when I went out on that dining porch. It was honed like a razor. I liked her, all right, if I was willing to cut a city man over her, but she just didn't seem like any kind of woman I thought I would ever find myself liking.

But she was good about those first rides home I gave her that summer. It was just a ride home, something I would do for anybody who didn't have a car. Corinne accepted it just that way. She didn't get all tight, like she was waiting for me to try something with her. And she didn't switch it all around and coo at me like she thought I gave her a ride just because she was a good-looking woman. She just accepted the ride, and thanked me for offering.

Out of the restaurant, she'd lean back in the car seat and tell me how she hated that long walk home after being on her feet all night. She said sometimes the public just seemed like one big hungry belly. She said the walk in to work wasn't so bad, with the sea breeze and the sunlight. But going back in the dark it seemed twice as far, and her arches ached and her legs felt like they were coming off at the thigh joints. She told me once, out of the blue, that I was the second-best cook in the world behind her mother.

I knew about having to walk after long shifts on my feet. I spent a lot of years without a car, too. Or with one that was always broken down, which is almost worst, because you never could count on it. That's why I appreciated that 1955 Chev of mine so good. In four years it had never let me down once. It was the only expensive new thing I ever owned, not counting my chef's cutlery.

I told Corinne she should try to buy a car. She told me that she thought about nothing else, but two kids in school with no child support from their fathers took a lot of money. Even living with her parents she never could seem to get any money ahead because she had to put money on household expenses.

She had been doing all right in Georgia. She had a job at an Army arsenal stitching artillery covers during the war years and stayed on through Korea. Then her father retired from the city fire department. He was determined to move to Florida because that's where you were supposed to retire to back then. She liked the idea too, because her grandmother thought Florida elementary schools were better than Georgia's. They turned out to be better, Corinne said, so she was glad they had moved even if there were no government jobs for her.

She never complained. Not even about her long walks home at night. The way she told it, they were epic treks like in a movie. She talked about her life like it was a movie, come to think of it, or something for other people to envy. The way she told it, maybe she was right. I know I got where I looked forward to driving her home. I wondered if she looked forward to it, too.

Once, I had been called small and dapper. Lately, I was just small. Maybe an inch taller than Corinne. I caught myself thinking about what I looked like to Corinne and tried to stop. A few more years of hot kitchens and Florida sun and I would be small and wrinkled, and wouldn't have to worry about what women thought of me.

God, what a place to grow old in! Tourists and retirees

can have it, believe me.

Before we knew for sure about Christine's TB, Chris and I had talked about maybe breaking loose and moving to New Orleans. Christine's people originally came from around there. I even thought about the part of the West Coast I saw in my post-war Army service. But all that kind of got lost after we knew about the TB. Now I was at Dawson's and Chris was in the sanatorium, and Sally was with her parents, and the days kind of ran together a lot of the time.

I worked it out once, and figured that since we moved to Florida my life had become too adjusted to tourist seasons. Like everybody who ever ended up on the Beaches, I had seen too many seasons roll by without ever getting rich, and finally without much hope for anything better.

The whole philosophy of the Beaches was just to survive more tourist season. Just one season that was fat, and then you could say screw it all and get out. Go somewhere with trees whose leaves turn pretty colors in the fall. But too many tourist seasons strung together without the big Quiniella falling on your number and finally it was too late to hope, and you were stuck in Florida for keeps. Since I left St. Pete, I had lived mostly because it seemed like too much of an effort to muster up to die.

Lately, though, life seemed better. Corinne was why. I didn't really understand that she was why until Dawson said he wasn't going to close after August. Corinne would be one of the waitresses staying on. I was surprised by how good that made me feel. It made the months after August something to look forward to more than anything I had in a long time.

Chapter Four

Once we knew that we would be working after August, my taking Corinne home got to be an understood thing. Nobody yet had started making remarks like they always do about anything at all between a man and a woman, no matter how innocent.

We talked about Dawson's chances of making money after August. Everybody at Dawson's talked about that. The people from the Blue Dolphin and the Jade were talking about it, too. Times were changing on the Beaches, but people who had lived with tourist seasons all their lives distrusted interruptions in the rhythm.

It was after Labor Day when she asked me to teach her how to drive a stick-shift car.

We had just finished one of the new short eight-hour shifts, down from the summer twelves. She had been reading the Florida driver's manual and said she was going to buy a car as soon as she could get her license and save the money. But she knew she couldn't afford an automatic transmission model.

I told her sure, I'd show her how to drive a stick shift.

She wanted to know when.

"Right now, if you want to," I said.

So instead of taking her straight home that night, I took her out on Penman Road and let her get under the wheel. She stalled the Chev three times before she managed to bump us along, riding the clutch, half a block.

The first time she tried to grab second, she almost got reverse and ground the gear teeth pretty bad. She panicked and backed off into neutral with her foot on the gas. That big old V-Eight let out a bellow and I got excited and yelled at her to get her damn foot off the gas. She tried to get it back into first gear, and it sounded like she had ripped the whole gearbox loose. Then she slammed on the brakes and I nearly went down in the floorboards under the dash. At least she had got off the accelerator.

She looked at me.

"Jesus Christ!" I said.

"These gears aren't right," she said.

"There's nothing wrong with the car," I said.

I didn't like her criticizing my car. I didn't mind helping her out, but if she was going to tear the damn clutch out, it didn't seem right for her to badmouth it, too.

"The gears are all wrong," she said again. She said it in that same flat voice she used when she was arguing with the other waitresses. It was the first time she had used it on me.

"Listen," I said. "They're *not* in the wrong damn place..."

"What kind of car is this, anyway?"

That stopped me. If she didn't even know cars apart, it was a cinch she had never been behind a steering wheel before.

"It's a Chevrolet," I said. "I thought you knew all about cars except gearshifts."

"I never told you *that*," she said. "I don't know nothing about cars except that they're better than walking and you have to know the gearshift. I told you I've driven one before. *One!*"

"Did it have gears?"

"I bet it had more than this one!" It was like she had won the argument.

"That's not the point. What *kind* of car?"

"It was a Plymouth, a 1937 Plymouth, and it didn't just have this little dooflingy on the steering wheel. It had a *real* gearshift."

I couldn't keep up with her. "What are you talking about now?"

"The gearshift was on the *floor*, just like on city busses!" she said, like that should shut me up for good.

I was through being mad. I wanted to laugh. I thought laughing at her was a bad idea right then. Of course I couldn't fool her.

"What's so funny all of a sudden?"

"You're absolutely right," I said. "You're talking about a *real* gearshift."

"Of course I'm right. My brother let my drive the panel truck he drives for that parts house in Macon, too, before we moved down here. I drove one car and one *truck,* if you must know. The truck had a real gearshift on the floor, too. It was a Dodge, if you must know. D-O-D-G-E. Just like Dodge City, on *Gunsmoke* on TV."

"Let's start again," I said. "Here's where first is, and here's second, and here's third. This up here is reverse. That's why it scraped. You tried to put it in reverse going forward. It's really the same gear-pattern, it just seems different because the knob sticks out to the side."

"Reverse," she said. "That's why it scraped."

"Yeah."

Headlights were coming up behind us.

"Wait until this car goes by and we'll try again," I said.

The car came up alongside and stopped. It was a dark blue Plymouth Fury with a white five-pointed star painted on the door.

"You folks havin' trouble?" The driver was a big, big-hatted shadow behind the steering wheel. His voice was soft in the night, but big too.

"No trouble, Billy," I said. "I'm just trying to show her how to use a gearshift."

"Oh--that you, Walter?"

"Yeah," I said.

"Dawson's started closing early, huh?"

"Uh-huh."

"Gettin' much city trade by staying open?"

"Not yet."

"Word'll get around." The big hat shifted slightly. "Is Walter teachin' you good, Miss?"

"It's *Mrs.*," she said, cold as ice on the Ohio River in February. "I'm beginning to catch on."

The hat shifted again. "Nice night for it. Maybe you should try workin' his gearshift out by the jetties. Less traffic."

"Thank you ever so much for your suggestion." Still the freeze.

Billy kind of chuckled. "Evenin', *missus*. You too, Wally."

"See you, Billy," I said. He pulled on down the road.

"Uppity cop!" she snapped.

"Billy's just being polite," I said. "That was the town marshal, not a cop. He doesn't like the word cop."

"Well he sure ain't no cowboy, even with that hat. I know what he is, and you know what? What he likes is tough titty. Where I come from we call a spade a spade, and a cop a cop."

"Billy's just a good old guy who sometimes jumps to conclusions."

"Like what?"

"Like he doesn't believe we're just out here to teach you to change gears."

"Why, that *son-of-a-bitch*," she said. The perfect outrage in her voice tickled me, and I started smiling again.

Her tone pretty much put me in my place, or showed me I didn't even rate having a place, but still it tickled me. She could be so perfectly high and mighty without even trying. Like that queen in the storybook: off with his head, the son-of-a-bitch!

She got the gears pretty well straightened out in her mind that night, and then I drove her home. She wasn't ready yet to try driving through town. But she was over the nerves and ready to do more driving, now she had the hang of it, if I would let her. I said sure, and she was kind of quiet, and bubbly as a kid just before Christmas, when I let her off. I was halfway back to my place before I realized I pretty much felt the same way myself.

Chapter Five

Once Corinne got the hang of driving, it was like dope to her. She couldn't get enough of it. That was fine with me, because it meant I could buy a six-pack and just sit in the passenger seat and ride. One thing that I had loved to do ever since I was a teenager was to ride around at night and drink beer. Between the end of tight money in the Depression and the start of gas rationing in the war, I never did get my fill of it.

I didn't like to drive when I was drinking, I just liked to ride. It had been a long time since I had been friends with anybody who liked to drive just to be driving. I guess it was a kid trick and they all grew up on me. And then I moved to Florida on top of that.

After August, Corinne drove me all over those beaches, as far north as Atlantic Beach and as far south as the Oasis Restaurant, which sat right on the beach sand just south of Ponte Vedra. We covered every street in between. About two nights a week we'd go riding after work. We worked six nights a week, but only the eight-hour shifts. Business was way off and the waitresses were taking turns getting off way before the restaurant closed. Corinne would work late the nights she wanted to drive around. Dawson was even talking about starting up a five-day week, just like an office, so everybody could get some hours in and two days at a time off. When Dawson got started breaking tradition, he was hard to stop.

The kitchen was like a tomb, almost. It was getting where I could finish all the Ellery Queen and Alfred Hitchcock and Mike Shayne mystery magazines by the middle of the month, and had to start buying paperbacks again. It got so slow I would occasionally sneak one of the girls' *True Confessions* off to the john. I must have read everything right down to all the classified ads in the Jacksonville evening paper every night.

One night was really bad. From seven to eight p.m. there wasn't a single customer. It was three weeks into September. The first full-moon tide had got the marsh hen hunting off to a good start, but everything else outdoors was dead, even the bluefishing. Dawson was going to go marsh hen shooting on the morning high tide, so he said what the hell and told us all to shut up early and go home.

Corinne had that look like let's go drive up a tank of gas, and I was ready.

"Let's go riding," I said.

She was just like a kid. "You really want to?"

"Let's go. We've got all night, and I can already taste the beer,"

I drove by the package store, got two six packs at the drive-in window and then got out of the car and went around. She slid over.

"Watch out for the county fuzz," the drive-in guy, Eddy, told me. "They're keeping an eye on the drive-ins. Easy pickin's, you know."

"Right," I said. I got out my church key and popped one open. It foamed up and made little bubble-bursting sounds.

"Just be careful," Eddy said.

"It doesn't matter," Corinne said, looking up at him. "I don't drink. I just drive."

He did a double take. "Come again?"

"Let's go, Corinne," I put in. "Good night, Eddy."

She pulled out. "What's so funny now?" she wanted to know.

I was grinning. I drank off half the can in two long swallows and slid down in the seat. I felt good.

"Don't try to tell people things they are never in a million years going to believe," I said. "It makes them think that you think they're stupid and they get mad with you."

"What would he never in a million years believe?"

"That you just want to go driving, and never have a beer. You can't expect a package store guy to believe that."

"Well it's none of his business anyway," she said.

We turned onto A1A and started down toward Ponte Vedra. The moon was almost full, fat and silver and a little lopsided now, just like a tropic moon in a Technicolor movie.

"He was just trying to be friendly," I said. "Sometimes the county deputies will charge you even if you're not drinking, if there's open stuff in the car."

"They can't do that," she said. She always kept both hands firmly on the wheel at the ten o'clock and two o'clock position, and her full attention on the road. "That's against the law," she added. It was, too, in those days.

"Honey," I said, "*they* are the law."

"My name's not Honey," she said to the windshield. "And no they ain't the law, either."

"Well, if they ain't, who is?"

"The Constitution of the United States," she said grandly, like a Catholic calling on Mary.

I laughed.

"You think that's funny?" she said in her dangerous voice.

I finished the beer and lobbed the can out into the ditch. We were coming into the long double row of expensive houses along both sides of A1A where Ponte Vedra started. I opened another.

"You sound like a barracks lawyer," I said.

"I know what that is. I saw it in a movie about the Army. That's a soldier who knows all the regulations and makes the sergeants go by them."

"Not exactly," I said. "They don't make anybody do anything. They can't, because they're nothing but soldiers. Mostly they just try to hide behind the regulations to get out of things they don't want to do."

"You think I'm trying to hide behind the Constitution of the United States?"

"I just had a picture of you pulling that crap about the Constitution of the United States on a county deputy."

"What do you mean?"

"You really don't think he'd pay any attention to that crap, do you?"

"He'd better, by God! He is a public servant, and he'd better act like one, or he won't be one for long."

"What if he told you to get out and walk a straight line?"

"I'd tell him to go straight to hell."

We rode a way farther. The houses got bigger and more spread out. Almost every one of them had two Cadillacs or sometimes an Oldsmobile or a Lincoln Continental parked in front. Rich Floridians didn't drive foreign cars in those days.

"I believe you would tell them that," I said finally.

"The law is to protect innocent citizens, not harass them!"

"All right," I said. I finished my second beer, tossed out the can and got another from the floorboards.

"I wish you wouldn't do that," she said.

"What?"

"Throw those beer cans on people's lawns."

"It don't hurt 'em any. They're rich. Most of 'em have a permanent yard man."

"So what? How would you like it if they threw cans in your yard?"

"I'd never notice," I said. Here she went in another

direction, defending the poor defenseless rich.

"Just because you wouldn't mind it doesn't mean they don't. You still shouldn't do it."

"All right, I give up," I said.

I liked her to take me in hand that way. It made it even better than just riding and drinking the beer. That was great, but it was even better when she started trying to re-raise me according to Georgia standards of conduct. She was pretty stubborn, but this time I was betting she couldn't change my ways very much. I never told her I was betting against her, though. Knowing there were odds against it would have really got her started on me.

I tossed my third can on the floorboards in back. She just nodded and smiled, and I was glad I had. Before I was half-through my fourth can, we were down at the Oasis.

"Stop a while," I said.

She looked at her watch. "All right. Fifteen minutes." She wheeled us over into the far side of the parking lot. I had already taught her about not trying to drive on soft sand.

"You sound like you're on a timetable," I said.

"My daddy waits up for me," she said. Her tone of voice closed the subject. I looked out at the ocean.

Remember all the old romantic tourist crap about a Florida moon on the Atlantic? It isn't crap. It especially isn't crap when you're beginning to feel the result of drinking too many beers too close together, and you're with a woman on a deserted beach. Sometimes that silver on the moving water can just get to you.

After Christine and Sally were gone, I used to drive to the Oasis after work to sit and think and keep from going back to that empty apartment. Sometimes, sober, the night ocean was almost too much to look at. I would leave and head for an all-night truck stop where everybody knew me and played a lot of loud jukebox music.

Tonight, though, I was protected from that kind of lonesome feeling because I was with Corinne. It made the moonlight all right again. It was like it had been waiting here all those other times to look at it through the beer with her there in the dark behind the steering wheel.

"It sure is pretty," I said.

"Ben used to tell me that I should see the moon come up behind those Oklahoma hills where he was born," she said. "Ben was my first husband. He was a real cowboy, had a horse and everything. There was a song out called *Those Oklahoma Hills Where I Was Born*. When he sang it, he sounded just like Ernest Tubb. He said kiyotes yodeled at the moon out there just like in the Westerns movies."

"What did you say back?"

She snorted, but not with the usual energy. "I told him the moon was just as pretty over the backyard of 1617 Central Way."

"Where's that?"

"In Macon, Georgia."

"Is the moon as pretty over 1617 Central Way as it is right here?"

She started to say something and then shut her mouth. It was like she was trying to get what she was saying exactly right.

"Well it was pretty, even in Macon. But I don't go for that romantic hogwash."

I just sipped my beer. I felt almost lost in that hammered silver radiance on the water. I read something once about silversmiths and hammered silver. The moon on the water looked just like hammered silver sounds, if it meant something to break your heart just to look at it.

Finally, she said, "Well?"

"Well, what?" I said.

"Well, what have you got to say to that?" She wanted

backtalk. Maybe she wanted to be argued into how pretty the moon was over the ocean. To hell with her.

"Where you think the moon is pretty from is your own business," I said.

"But I never thought of it as all that pretty, even over Macon! Not the way he was talking about it."

The moonlight and the beer and her warm soft presence in the car was so different from her complaining voice. I was in a rare mood, all right.

"But he wanted to impress you with how pretty it was where he came from, and you just had to put him in his proper place." I was feeling old and sad and drunk.

She started to say something again, and stopped. This time she kept still. I liked her a lot better that way. I got kind of lost in the moon-dazzle on the ocean. The burning moonlight really had a grip on me, and the feel of a woman sitting quietly beside me in the shadows of the car.

"Walter," she said, after a long while.

"What?" I said.

"We better start back. Daddy..."

"All right," I said. The relaxed feeling was slipping away, and I couldn't seem to hold onto it. I let it go. "All right," I said again.

Chapter Six

The second weekend in October I went over to see Christine and Sally and the in-laws. Sally was doing real well in school. Sally's grandparents thought it was smart to leave her there. She was adjusting beautifully, the school principal told me. That's the word he used, beautifully. I called him up at home to ask about her. He thought I was doing the right thing, to let her stay in school there, and asked if I had ever considered moving inland. I told him my kind of job needed the big tourist restaurants on the coast to pay me enough to keep Christine and Sally going. He said it must be hard to be separated from them all the time and I said yes it was.

Sally's grandparents had really done her up fine for school clothes with the money I sent. I thought they must have put some of their own money there, too, because all her stuff looked so nice. I didn't mention it and neither did they. They were good for Sally, and she loved them. They had always thought I was okay, and they admired me for sticking it out at Dawson's for the money we needed for Chris. Chris's old man was so disorganized he couldn't find the john without knowing the missus was around somewhere. That's what he called her, the missus.

Chris just looked tired and worn-out. She looked old. She never had been a real looker, just slim and neat and quiet. Now she looked like she must be over fifty years old, and more skinny than slim. She looked too tired even to die.

She was kind of distant about everything, the way sick people and shut-ins are. Those were the last days that the rest-cure still was considered the top treatment for TB victims, but the drug discoveries were coming on strong.

She said the drugs made her too sick and weak to think. But the doctors told me that she was doing fine and would be strong enough for short visits home in the spring, maybe, if the drugs kept working and the TB didn't bounce back. Even the idea of getting out of the sanatorium for a while didn't seem to cheer her up. She had lost all her points of reference. She seemed almost relieved when I got ready to leave her room. It was as if the strain of trying to follow whatever I was talking about was just too much of a burden.

I guess it was like being in the Army. After I was in the Army for a while everything you had been before, like your childhood, was over and wasn't ever coming back. I sometimes said I spent about a thousand years in the Army during my two-year hitch in between V-J Day and Korea.

I drove straight back to the Beaches on Sunday afternoon without stopping to eat. That was before Interstate 10 was finished as far as Lake City. Sixty miles an hour was pushing it on old U.S. 90, and I pushed it all the way back. That Chev of mine was a thoroughbred. That V8 seemed to wake up and purr when I got it up and running out there on the highway, after all my putting around on the Beaches. I blew a lot of carbon out of the exhaust on the way home and that was good for that big engine too.

It was an overcast kind of blurry day without any shadows or any definite clouds when I hit the Beaches, but there was a good wind blowing off the ocean. It almost felt like it might be the first good Northeaster of the season. It felt good.

There was a new movie on at the Jacks Beach Theater. When I stopped at Dawson's for my next week's work schedule, I asked Corinne if she wanted to go to the eight-thirty show. She was working the same screen porch where she'd hit that guy. The ocean porch always closed first when business was slow. She looked kind of nervous about my asking and I thought she was going to say no. But she said all right.

"How long does it last?" she said.

"It should be out by ten," I said.

"Okay."

"You want to go home and get changed, and me pick you up?"

"No," she said, real quick. "It's just a movie. I'll just go in my uniform, and then straight home."

I was disappointed. After the time over there with Chris, I felt depressed. I would like to have gone to the movie and then taken Corinne somewhere to eat somebody else's cooking besides mine. But at least she'd said yes to the movie.

I forget exactly which movie it was. It was one of those big ones they spent more money to make than I could imagine, and had a whole lot of big-name stars in it. The newspapers had been whooping it up for months before it even got to Jacksonville, let alone out to the Beaches. When we got to the theater, though, there was no line at all at the ticket booth and the house was only half full.

Beachites are real funny about movies. Corinne's view of Beachites was that everybody on the Beaches was the dregs of humanity, washed up there to rot. A lot of them came from other places, all right. What would draw a big crowd in L.A. or Chicago or New York would get this on the Beaches.

I used to think Beach people would be happier if the movie house just charged them to come in and sit and stare at the blank screen, like you do before the movie starts. People on the Beaches didn't want a movie to be too funny or too clever or too sad, or too anything. They didn't want to have to pay close attention to keep from missing anything. They would get up and walk out if it was too predictable. They wanted a good even keel in their movies, just like they wanted in their daily lives. I figured that a blank screen with half-lighting and Muzak in the background would come closest to all they wanted in a film.

I liked movies, and wanted them to be all kinds. Corinne turned out to want them to be romantic and for the good guys always to win. We enjoyed that movie more than the crowd did, and talked about it all the way to where I dropped her off at the foot of her street. As I remember, the good guys did win. I don't remember the romance part, but I remembered the good feeling from going to the movie with her long after I forgot what movie it was.

The good feeling of the movie got me as far as a bar I knew on First Street called the Blue Lamp, and held me until I had half-a-dozen drafts in me. Then I shot pool on the quarter-a-game table with some sailors off an aircraft carrier and a party boat skipper that I sort of knew. We played for beers. I won four and paid for three when I lost.

The beer and the pool got me home and to bed. The next thing I knew the phone was ringing. It was Mabel, and I was back in the rut again.

Chapter Seven

*I*t was later in October when Mabel told me one day that Dawson wanted to see me. I was just coming on shift. It was two p.m. and we had the whole night ahead of us. It must be something special or he would have just come on back after I had relieved the lunch staff and had the kitchen sorted out to tell me what was on his mind.

I went through the main dining room and down the little hall to the restrooms and Dawson's office. His door was open, cigarette smoke trailing out into the still air of the hall. He was reading some stuff on his desk.

"Hi, Walter," he said.

"Mabel said you wanted to see me."

"Yep. Close that door, will you?"

His voice sounded funny, like a voice gets when it has a load on its tongue just waiting to be dumped. I closed the door.

"Thanks," he said. He was reading the stuff on his desk again. "Sit down, Walter, I'll just be a minute."

I sat on the small sofa chair in front of his desk. I wondered if he'd changed his mind about the TB. I had worked the first few months expecting that at any time. It just didn't seem right he could wait this long to change his mind about that. I wondered if the cops from Tampa had found out where I worked and put in a word with the Duval County health department. Then I wondered if one of the bus boys had accused me of stealing food. That happened once years ago when I was a short order cook in an all-night joint in Cincinnati. The boss believed me instead of the bus boy, who finally broke down and confessed it was him stealing the food. But I had been scared, because that's how bad rumors started. In this business a bad reputation could kill you. My palms felt damp now, just remembering. No, not remembering. I was scared now.

Dawson shoved the papers aside and lit up another of his Camels. "How's Chris, Walter?" he said.

"She's all right. Getting a little better. She may be able to come home for visits in the spring. She's all right."

"Glad to hear it. And Sally?"

"Sally is fine. Her grandparents are spoiling her rotten. She's perfect. She's okay."

"Spoiling her, huh? You know, that's what our Ginny says we do to her boys. She's right, probably. Why not? Why the hell not? Even my grandkids won't be young forever."

"Not even long enough," I said.

I got a lump in my throat, thinking how Sally changed between the times I saw her. I swallowed and tried to concentrate, because I knew he didn't call me to the office to talk about kids. He could have done that in the kitchen later. He always had before. He had mentioned Chris right off the bat, but didn't blink when I said she might be staying with me in the spring. It didn't fee like this was about Chris.

"By the way." He blew a careful smoke ring at the ceiling.

Here it came, whatever it was.

"By the way," he said again, "I hear you're seeing Corinne."

So that was it. I stood up.

"I'll be in the kitchen."

"Now, wait." He knocked ash, hung the Camel in his lip and folded his hands on the desk. He was a big man. He was over six feet tall, broad and big-boned. The Florida outdoors and restaurant work agreed with him. Me standing and him sitting didn't make him look one bit smaller or less impressive, not at all.

I cleared my throat. "That's none of your business, Mr. Dawson," I said.

He kind of narrowed his eyes and his mouth thinned out. He had a big head and it was mostly bald. All the skin on his head was deep bronze from the sun. His hands were big and hard from years of hanging on by his fingernails. His eyes could be hard. They were hard now.

"Don't get tough with me, Walter," he said through the Camel. He was the one who looked tough. Damned tough. "I don't need your getting tough with me."

"I'm not trying to be tough," I said. I hadn't expected anything like this. " It's just that's my business, that's all."

"Let me say my say before you decide that," Dawson said.

"What I do on my own time is my own business." I cleared my throat again, hating it that I had to. I was scared, but he had to understand that my business was my own.

"All *right*, Goddammit!" He stubbed out the butt like he wished it was my neck. "Did I say different? I don't deserve this crap from you, Walter. Don't get so Goddamn uppity with me! I'm trying to tell you something that might keep you from getting hell beat out of you."

That got through to me.

"You're not trying to tell me to lay off seeing Corinne?"

"I'm trying to tell you it might be a good idea. Now, wait!" He held up one of those big hands like a cop stopping traffic. "*Listen*, will you?"

"All right," I said.

"Sit down, then."

I sat back down and he looked me over like he had never seen me before.

"You're some feisty little rooster, ain't you?"

"I mind my own business," I said.

"So do I. I hate my business being interfered with. I hate things to happen that hurt my business. If you get killed, that'll hurt business. If Corinne ups and quits, that'll hurt business because the customers really like her. Here I'm trying to stay open longer than I ever did before, and I don't want neither one to happen."

I was listening now. "Why should either one happen, though?" I said. "I mean, anybody can quit anytime. But especially that part about somebody getting killed?"

"You know Bill Ombear, guy runs the Derby House, don't you?"

"Just to speak to. Tough guy. Tough friends, too. Why?"

"That's where Corinne worked before she came here."

"I know that."

"She tell you why she came here?"

"To work for the famous Dawson's Seafood Restaurant."

"That's flattering, but it ain't the truth," Dawson said. "Not all of it, anyway. Bill Ombear had the hots for her. Ombear's buddy Rennie Cross got him started on her. Rennie used to hang around with Corinne's old man, going deep-sea fishing, drinking, like that. Rennie made a pass at Corinne and she shot him down like she always does. Then he started in after her at work over at the Derby. Bill hadn't paid any attention to her before then."

"Ombear's got a reputation with women," I said.

Dawson nodded at me. "Bill usually has plenty of stuff on tap, but he got to looking Corinne over and told Rennie to buzz off, he wanted some of that for himself. Then Bill told Corinne she was gonna be his new skirt. She told him to go to hell just exactly the same way she told Rennie. Ombear got mad as hell and told her it was fuck or be fired."

I was tight all over now, and now I really was scared. The crowd that hung out at the Derby was a rough bunch. I was sick, too, in the pit of my stomach. I could tell she had got to be pretty important to me by then, because the thought somebody like Ombear just taking her over like that made me feel like throwing up.

It had gone on right here on the Beaches, too, and everybody knowing but me. Everybody laughing at me riding around with her all the time, and waiting for Ombear to catch me at it, beat the crap out of me. He was a mean son of a bitch.

All for a Roman holiday. That was one of Corinne's sayings from her mother: all for a Roman holiday. It meant the way people will run six blocks to see the fresh blood in a car wreck or to watch a house burn down with everything a family owns inside.

This all ran through my mind in way less time than it takes to write it down. I had to say something. Dawson was waiting.

"So she's Ombear's property, huh?" I said.

"Oh hell no," Dawson said. "That piece of shit? No, you still don't understand, Walter. We could handle Ombear. *I* can handle Ombear. We could make him lay off or even call the cops if we had to. Not that I had to when we were both in high school. I kicked his ass then and I could now. But they don't like Ombear much, the cops. They'd be happy to dance him around a little if I asked. Corinne didn't go down for him, Walter."

The sickness went away so fast I was dizzy. "She didn't?"

"No. She just walked right out of there and called a cab and went home. She was so mad she wasn't thinking, because when her daddy asked her why she was home early, she told him. He blew his stack and jumped in his car and drove up there and went after Ombear right in his own restaurant. Rennie was there."

"I don't remember hearing anything about this," I said.

"You wouldn't have. You were probably off somewhere minding your own business."

"All right, all right," I said. "Didn't the police do anything?"

"They said he had it coming."

"Why, those pricks." I was getting mad now. "That bastard Ombear--"

"That's exactly what the cops said," Dawson said. "Let me finish."

I just looked at him.

"Corinne's old man nearly killed Ombear," he said, grinning. "He broke Ombear's nose and cracked two ribs and knocked at least one tooth out. He beat Ombear so bad he was in the hospital for a week and some of those scars are going with him to his grave. Rennie tried to stop Corinne's old man, and he hit Rennie once. Once. He knocked him cold. He said the next son-of a-bitch he caught messing with his daughter was going to get his balls cut off and fed to the seagulls."

I couldn't take it all in. "Her *daddy* did that? Mr. Valland? He's retired!"

"He's a retired city fireman from Macon, Georgia," Dawson said. "They called him Bull ever since he broke a grown man's jaw when he was fifteen. He is absolutely as mean as they come, Walter. And from what I heard today, Bull figures that the next son-of-a-bitch messing with his daughter is you."

"Oh," I said.

There didn't seem to be a lot else to say.

Chapter Eight

The evening after Dawson talked to me, Corinne came back to the kitchen after the first dinner rush and drew a cup of coffee and stood around like she had something on her mind too. I wondered if Dawson had talked to her too. I was still trying to figure out what to think about what he had told me.

"You goin' to be around the Beaches this weekend?" she said.

"I guess so. I'm supposed to play poker Friday night. Why?"

"Mama wants you to come for dinner," she said. "Daddy got her a new barbecue grill for their anniversary. She's gonna fix some hamburgers and stuff."

You just never knew which direction Corinne was going to come from next.

"Well," I said. I thought about Ombear in the hospital and about Rennie knocked out with one punch. "I don't know, " I said finally. "I wouldn't want to intrude."

"You ain't intruding. I'm inviting you."

"Does your daddy know you are?"

"What's that got to do with it?"

"I don't want to intrude on people who can beat up Bill Ombear and Rennie Cross in the same fight," I said.

Her face got tight. "Look: I do what I want to do. I'm a grown woman. I'm thirty years old. Ombear got way out of line and if Daddy had of let me calm down first, I would have gone back and taken care of that son-of-bitch myself."

"Bill Ombear? How?"

"I would have cut his heart out, by God. But Daddy

just blew up and took off. Ombear got lucky because somebody got Daddy to stop. But if you're afraid of Daddy, don't worry. He's going fishing Saturday and won't be back home until late."

The way she said that got my goat. "I'm not afraid."

"All right. I'll tell Mama you're coming for sure, then. I told both of them you were a nice guy. Daddy thinks you're crazy to let a woman drive your new car. He only let me drive that Plymouth of his once and swore never again. Mama never learned how. He don't like women driving. She never drove teams of horses when he was young and he don't see no difference."

"All right, I'll be there," I said. "I'll wear my glasses, though."

"That wouldn't make no difference if he started after you," she said. "Don't get smart."

"Not me."

She finished her coffee and went back on the floor and left me wondering what the hell I was getting into now. I wasn't sure I wanted to be presented to the parents of a thirty-year-old woman. We just drove around so that I got to drink beer and she got to drive. That was all. It was simple and I liked it and would miss it if she quit going riding with me. I had enjoyed going to that movie with her, too.

Now it was getting more complicated. I wondered what Chris would say if she knew I was going to visit another woman's parents on the weekend. To hell with it. It was just grilled hamburgers in the backyard. I might as well go.

I could go and eat their hamburgers and be polite and then leave. I was just letting Corinne drive my car until she got her license, that was all. It was nothing. These Georgians meant nothing to me, and I wasn't after their daughter. Besides, I was a grown man. Way past grown. I didn't have to answer to anybody. And Corinne was a grown woman who could ask whoever she wanted over for hamburgers. I might as well go. It might look bad if I didn't. They might get their Georgia feelings hurt. That would really be something, if I didn't go and Bull Valland came and beat hell out of me for insulting their hospitality.

It was my first what you'd call social contact with deep-dyed Georgians. I wasn't sure what might set them off. All right, I would go.

Chapter Nine

I was pretty nervous when I turned the Chev up Corrine's street that Saturday. She lived on one of those little lanes that run in from First Street and dead-end against the big oceanfront properties. It was about three in the afternoon when I stopped in front of the house.

It was an old white beach-style garage apartment converted into a two-story house with green trim. The green roof had a lot of pitches and angles, and there were screened porches taking up half the top and bottom floors on the ocean side. It looked like there would never be a night too hot to sleep cool on those porches. Like all those houses crammed up close behind the seawall, the house took up almost every foot of the lot it sat on, but there was room to park half-off off the lane in front. Rows of roof-high palm trees ran down both sides, with the fronds close enough to scrape the upstairs windows. I thought sleeping upstairs might be like sleeping in Tarzan's tree house.

I parked in front. Across the street was a vacant lot that had been cut down except for the palm trees and wild Spanish bayonet. Two young boys with toy bows and arrows were using some cardboard boxes for target practice. The arrows made a kind of *boof* sound when they hit the boxes. The oldest one grabbed a box and threw it straight up as far as he could.

"Get it!" he yelled.

I was out of the car and stopped to watch. The younger boy drew and released. The arrow hit the flying box, but without the solid *boof* sound. There was a kind of clank and flutter and the arrow glanced off. The sun glinted along its wooden shaft. It came lobbing over toward the house, wobbling. It seemed to fall in slow motion.

I put out my hand as the arrow fell past and caught it out of the air.   The bigger kid was right behind it, running, looking scared. He stopped so fast he almost tipped over. We looked at each other. Then he looked at the house. I looked, too.

There were three round fluffs of first-aid cotton poked into the screen door at the front of the house. Where they went through the screen, they were squeezed down to the size of the arrow's shaft. We looked at each other again. I handed him the arrow.

Corinne came out through the screen door. She was in a white blouse and a pleated plaid skirt and loafers. It was the first time I had seen her not in a waitress uniform. Something funny happened to my breathing for a minute.

She looked at the boy holding the arrow. "You're just going to keep on," she said.

"Aw, Corinne—it was an *accident!*"

"I told you not to shoot toward the house."

"We didn't! We didn't! The arrow just bounced. Honest. Ask him!"

She looked at me. "Hello, Walter."

"Hi," I said.

She sighed. "All right, where did it hit the screen this time?"

"It didn't," I said.

"So you're Walter," the kid said. He was maybe twelve, and not very impressed.

"This is my oldest son, Ben," Corinne said. I wondered why he called her by her first name, but didn't say anything.

"Hello, Ben."

He didn't say anything at all, just kept staring at me.

"That over there is Little Luke," Corinne said.

The younger one looked like a blond Cupid in

dungarees and a T-shirt. Maybe seven, maybe eight. He hadn't moved since he let the arrow go. His face was expressionless, waiting for whatever was going to happen.

"You get them boxes up," Corinne told both of them. "It's time to eat."

I could smell charcoal smoke and grilling meat by then. Corinne looked back at me when Ben ran back across the lane. "You hungry?"

"Yes," I said.

"Play poker last night?"

"Til five this morning."

"Jesus. Win anything?"

"A few dollars,"

"Well, come on back. Mama's back there."

We went through a tiny living room full of worn rattan furniture, an even smaller kitchen with an old-fashioned cast-iron sink and then out through a dining room that opened on the back yard. Corinne's mother was a stooped, frail woman with bobbed hair the color of iron shavings and clear blue eyes. Corinne must take after Bull, I thought. That didn't surprise me for some reason. Her mother called me Mister.

"Call me Walter," I said.

"Thank you," she said. "I hope you won't be too critical of my cooking, Walter."

"Not me," I said.

Mrs. Valland had a lovely Southern drawl, not hard-edged like Corrine's. Like mint juleps and plantations. Thank you for saying call me Walter. Like it was a nice little hostess gift I had given her. I liked her right away. She had what used to be called real style even stooped over from the years and in a faded print housedress.

Mrs. Valland reminded me of some of the retired women who wintered in the hotel I cooked for in Saint Pete. Those women all had money of course, comfortable retirements to back up their style. Plenty of them had the money but no style at all. The ones with style, though, made an impression. Maybe it was just me, but a lot of the ones I knew like that were Southern. A black doorman at the hotel, of all people, told me they were all that was left of the Southern aristocracy. That had a pretty ring to it and after that I always thought of the ones with style as Southern aristocracy. They had a gentle graciousness about them. Give Mrs. Valland a new dress and get her hair done, and she would have fit right in.

"Let's eat," she said. "Corinne, you get Ben and Little Luke. Walter, there are plates and silver and stuff on the table there."

Corinne went around the house. I could hear her yelling. "Beeyuun! Luke! C'mon! Dinnertime!"

I went over to get a plate.

The hamburgers were grilled right and Mrs. Valland's French fries were hand sliced from fresh potatoes and weren't greasy. I hate frozen French fries and I hate greasy French fries. I never could talk Dawson into not using frozen for our fish and chips, but I could and did keep them from being greasy. People would have paid a premium for Mrs. Valland's fries. The iced tea was the best I had tasted in all my years in Florida. I hadn't even known iced tea could taste like that. I drank Dawson's iced tea in the kitchen because it was something cold and wet. I would rather have had a beer, but even Dawson wasn't that easy-going. If his tea had tasted like this, I might have given up beer.

"This is the best iced tea I have ever tasted," I said.

Mrs. Valland smiled. "More?"

I handed my glass over.

"Everybody says that about our tea," Corinne said. "It's true, too. That's because she uses fresh tealeaves, not bags, and she brews it fresh every day. Only chill it with ice cubes when you drink it. You never should keep tea in an icebox." Corinne called all refrigerators iceboxes. So did Mrs. Valland. It must have been a Georgia thing

"And you should never use aluminum pitchers," Mrs. Valland said. "I read in the paper where some brewery out west is putting beer in aluminum cans for pity sake. These new-fangled ways rob food and drink of its goodness." She handed me back the full glass.

All my years in kitchens and the Georgians were teaching me how to do it right. I found it charming as hell. We were sitting in cheap folding lawn chairs in the back yard. The back yard was a little wider than the house, and about twenty feet deep. There was an outdoor shower at one end, and a white-painted board table at the other. It was smeared with dirty brown stains and smelled faintly like fish. The yard was walled in for privacy by tall Spanish bayonet on all sides. Better than barbed wire. There were big shade trees in all the surrounding yards, and they broke the autumn sun off us. The oleander smell from next door, even this late in the year, was so thick you could almost bottle it right out of the air.

I drank some more iced tea.

"You want another hamburger?" Corinne asked me.

"No thanks," I said. "Two's plenty. Especially that size!"

"You're sure now?" Mrs. Valland said.

"Yes ma'am."

I felt good. The breeze off the ocean was ruffling the Spanish bayonet and the trees, and in one of the other yards a radio was tuned to an FM station playing scores from a Broadway musical, but not too loud. People over there were talking and laughing. You could hear the tinkle of ice cubes. A mocking bird was sitting on the outdoor showerhead and a big grey cat was stalking it from the shadows of the Spanish bayonet. The mocking bird ignored it. I could hear Ben and Little Luke shouting out front, and occasionally the twang of their bowstrings. They had eaten with the speed and silence of Apache warriors and gone back on the warpath.

"Corinne tells me you play poker," Mrs. Valland said.

"I play at it," I said.

"My father was a gambler," she said. She sounded like she thought a gambler was a fine thing to be.

"A professional gambler?"

"Not completely. He was a painting contractor, too, but he did play on the riverboats on the Savannah River until they stopped running. He loved it so. He really loved to go to those houses where they used to let you play Solitary against the house."

"Solitary?" I said.

"Solitaire," she said. "We call it Solitary in Georgia."

"I never heard of playing Solitaire in a gambling house."

"The house would charge you a dollar a card. You paid fifty-two dollars, and they broke open a new deck for you. The houseman would shuffle and let you cut, and then you played out the hand. You got five dollars back for every card you put up. Sometimes he could play all night without ever getting anywhere, but without losing tremendously. The most you could lose at a time was fifty-two dollars."

"Still a lot of money back then," I said.

She smiled. "Sometimes he would win. That's five times fifty-two, plus the house had a standing bonus of two hundred if you could do it. That's four hundred sixty dollars. He won a number of times, and *that* was a lot of money, then. He sometimes paid off his painters on a job from his winnings."

The storytelling rhythm was on her. I'd heard it from old folks growing up back in Ohio. This had that extra flavor of the Deep South to it.

"Your father sounds pretty colorful," I said, to keep her going.

"I was their youngest of seven," she said. She was gazing out toward the sound of the ocean, invisible from the back yard. "We had a good life, gambling and all, until Prohibition kicked in. My father did dearly love his whisky. He broke down and cried, I mean real tears, the night Prohibition went in. He just couldn't understand why people he had never heard of would do that to him. It was like the Reconstruction all over again, after the War."

Here we were a dozen years past World War Two in a little beach town in north Florida, but there was only one war that had been "the war" to a Georgian.

"Prohibition killed my father," Mrs. Valland said. "He got hold of some bad home likker. You know, moonshine most people call it. Made with lead pipe, and it half-paralyzed him. Some said the home likker was too much for him on top of all the lead in the paint. He died way before they repealed Prohibition. That's why I joined the rumrunners, to get him decent liquor in his illness."

I wasn't sure I had heard her right. "You were a rumrunner?"

She straightened her shoulders. "I was a flapper, Walter. Rumrunners had girlfriends, you know. And the police then would never have dared search a lady's purse for a gun or a rendezvous map."

"Mama," Corinne said. She sounded exasperated. I was trying to decide if her mother was spinning yarns to impress the Yankee or telling tales out of school. I never found out what Corinne was going to say, though.

A car came slamming up the lane from First Street and stopped out front. Car doors slammed to the sound of men's voices. I heard Ben call out Daddy's here and I forgot all about Prohibition and gun molls. My stomach did a nasty little twist around Mrs. Valland's good food. Ben and Little Luke called their grandparents Mama and Daddy in imitation of their mother.

I had almost forgotten about Bull Valland in the midst of Mrs. Valland's stories of the south. I wondered if she hadn't forgotten too, from the look of weariness that settled across her face and made her old again.

"He'll have a lot of fish to clean," she said. "He always does. Corinne, go get the knives and pans..."

"Mama! I've got a *guest!*" Corinne's face was set in angry lines.

"All right," the old woman said, and got up slowly.

I got up too. "Maybe I can help. I can fillet with the best of 'em."

"No," she said. "No, you're a guest. Corinne is right."

"Come on," Corinne said to me. "Let's walk down to the seawall."

"I-nezz!" came a loud male voice. "Where the hell *are* you?"

Mrs. Valland raised her voice. "I'm coming."

"Well, come *on*, then, God damn it..."

Bull Valland came around the side of the house lugging a pair of red snapper that must have weighed fifty pounds apiece. He stopped flat-footed when he caught sight of me. He wasn't as tall as I had expected. He wasn't any taller than me, but he was about three times as wide. He didn't have a shirt on, and the block of chest muscle and solid belly fat that passed for his body was brown as an Indian. His face looked like an Indian. Muscled and dark, like it had been born that way.

Standing there in his baggy shorts, holding those fish by the gills with his arms flexed to swing their tails clear of the ground, he looked like he was built out of some smooth brown metal. His biceps looked bigger and harder than a cantaloupe. I heard the screen door bang behind me. Mrs.

Valland was coming back with a big pan and knives.

Corinne said, "Daddy, this is Walter, from the restaurant."

"Hello, Mr. Valland," I said.

He looked at me. The look felt like it carried all the way through me, burned down the Spanish bayonet, and bounced off something way behind me.

Then he said, "Umph," and nodded, a single short jerk of his head, like a hatchet falling.

He turned toward the stained cleaning table and slipped one of the snappers smoothly up onto it. It seemed to take about as much effort as, say, laying a folded newspaper up there. Bill Ombear was one lucky son-of-a bitch to be alive.

"Inez!" he grumbled.

"I'm coming," she said quietly, and went on by me.

I couldn't take my eyes off him. He moved like some oiled, man-shaped machine. The big grey cat that had been stalking the mocking bird materialized beside the second snapper's tail. It reached up with a pawful of extended claws.

Valland seemed to sense it coming, and turned, lifting the fish out straight at arm's length. The cat started to stretch up after it. An instant too late its instincts warned it to duck. It was too slow. Bull had him. He held the cat dangling from his other hand, its big head cupped in his fist. I waited for a blur of claws to shred Bull's fist. The cat's big body curved up, hind claws reaching.

Bull's knuckled tightened.

The cat's body just froze and hung there, halfway arched up, not moving.

"Smart kitty," Bull laughed. He snapped his wrist and flipped the animal over the Spanish bayonet toward the partying sounds. As far as I saw, the cat didn't scratch him a single time.

There was an uproar of shouts, dogs barking, and charging sounds around the base of the Spanish bayonet. The cat shot back through the yard with a pair of enthusiastic Daschunds in hot pursuit. Bull laughed again, and nudged the second snapper onto the table beside the first.

"That you, Bull?" a woman called from next door.

"Nobody else, sweetheart!" he shouted back.

"Catch anything?"

"Don't ask damn fool questions, woman!"

"Who's that?" I asked Corinne.

"That's Leslie," Corinne said with a sneer in her voice I'd never heard. "One of his women."

"One of his..."

"C'mon," she said.

"Where?"

"To the beach, like I said."

"We're not going to help him?"

"He caught 'em, he can clean "em."

Her voice had a contempt I had never heard her use on anybody before. At the moment it seemed to include her mother for putting up with him.

We went around the house into the lane and turned up toward the seawall. Bull came around the far side of the house. There was a rusted old station wagon double-parked in the lane. A couple of men were sitting on the lowered tailgate, facing away from us. One of them was Rennie Cross, but he didn't see us. We walked on up the lane.

"Rennie Cross?" I said.

"He groveled, and Daddy let him back in the pack," Corinne said. "You ought to be around here tomorrow about noontime when all those fish guts start to really stink in the heat of the day. He fills up a whole garbage can. The garbage men don't come till Monday. Stinks bad enough to make you puke. Stinks so bad you can't even sleep on the porch."

"This goes on every weekend?"

"Weekends because his running buddies still got jobs. Yeah, every weekend except in winter. It's almost over for this year, thank God for small favors. As soon as this weather breaks, it'll be over. His cronies start going deer hunting over in central Florida. He doesn't do that. He hates deer meat. They try to get him to go, every year. They know he's the best shot of anybody except Ben, and I won't let them take Ben yet, he's too young, maybe never, not with those creeps. They want Daddy because he's such a good shot but he won't go. Summers is hell, though."

"Doesn't he ever get sick of fish?"

"Not him. He says why did we move to Florida for if we can't eat fish. He even eats them cold with his grits in the morning. Can you imagine that?"

"I can't imagine grits," I said.

"Don't get smart, Yankee," she said. But she was finally smiling again. Then she stopped. "He raises hell every time Mama wants a fryer for Sunday dinner, or a even a roast." She shook her head. "He's just plain crazy. Has been every since he retired."

"How old is he, anyway?"

"Fifty-eight."

"Jesus Christ!"

"What are you Jesus Christing about now?"

"If he looks like that now, what did he look like when he was thirty?"

"Just as ugly and just as mean." She wasn't joking, either.

The breeze on the seawall was cool, almost cold. It was low tide. Cars were cruising by down on the hard sand by the water. Some people out walking their dogs had coats on.

"Why did you ask me what he looked like when he was younger?" she said.

"He's in such good shape, is all."

"What, with that pot gut?"

I didn't think his hard round belly took anything away from Bull Valland's power. I didn't think many people would think so, including the woman next door. Bull Valland just filled up that back yard with the force of his presence. But by God he didn't draw much water with his own daughter.

In her way, she was just like him. But I wasn't going to say that to her. Not now or ever. She was his daughter, all right. It was the sweet-voiced mother who had been a flapper that I had a hard time seeing any resemblance to.

Chapter Ten

A week later I took Corinne to the Highway Patrol testing station in Jacksonville to take her driving test. Back then you had to take your written before you got your learner's permit and she already had a permit when she started driving with me. She already had the eye test done, too, so all she had to take was the driving test. She was nervous as hell. That license seemed to mean an awful lot to her. Instead of chattering the way most women do when they're nervous, she just clammed up. I don't remember a word being said all the way to Jacksonville. She was so quiet I began to get the fidgets, too.

The day was one of those bright clear days that are not cold and are not quite hot that passes for fall in North Florida. The weather had just begun to break that week and the ocean was acting up. I guessed Bull Valland would be about through fishing for this season and his buddies would be getting ready to go deer hunting. It was kind of nice to think about all those things the change in the weather would mean that I hadn't known about before. It was nice in a strange way to be having the fidgets along with her as I drove her to town. If I learned anything in my life it was that it was always better to be having the fidgets going toward something than a headache coming away from another night of nothing.

I knew Corinne could pass the test. She had turned out to be a good and careful driver. She was too careful but I thought she would get over that when she got some real experience. If she didn't get over it she would probably keep on poking along until some throttle-jockey clipped her. Then she would get over it or she would stop driving entirely. After she beat hell out of the throttle jockey of course. That would be Corinne, all right. One extreme or the other.

I was going to let her drive to town, but she didn't want to. I thought it would loosen her up, but she was holding herself together for the big effort. Every once in a while I glanced over at her. She was staring a hole right through the windshield. Her face was set like it had been frozen that way. The resemblance to Bull Valland was eerie. I had never noticed before that she had those high Indian cheekbones like he did.

I thought there must be real Indian blood in the Valland family, but I never wanted to ask. Cherokee, probably, since she said some of her folks hailed from North Carolina. But some of those Southern people took on as bad about Indian blood as they did about Negro blood. If you said anything about any kind of mixed blood to a Southerner, you weren't just asking, you were accusing. The righter you were, the faster you better be able to run. I thought there must be real Indian blood in there, though. It seemed too strong to just be a family mark. Those kids of Corinne's had it, too.

Neither one of her husbands had managed to thin it down much. Even though Little Luke was blond, I remembered the look on his face when the arrow he shot almost hit the house. The same look that Bull Valland gave me when he caught sight of me in his backyard.

Corinne had that look now. She was staring right at something that was about to happen, and was one hundred per cent ready to take it on with everything she had. Silly things like conversation or facial expression just went away. There was just a Valland and whatever that Valland was facing. This was a driving test, and Corinne was locked onto it like radar. I had been driving all my life so it was hard for me to grasp how big a thing getting this license was to her.

I read somewhere you can get too tense worrying about a thing. That you can get so tense just thinking about it that the thinking gets in the way of doing the thing itself. It sounded pretty good at the time. But it didn't apply to Corinne. I don't know why. It just didn't.

The testing station was part of a new Highway Patrol barracks that had opened just that year under the main viaduct that carried traffic up to the Fuller Warren Bridge. The barracks sat back off Riverside Avenue under the viaduct, and the hum of tires and roar of diesel trucks making the climb was steady when we got there about ten-thirty.

I wondered if the troopers who slept in the barracks thought the constant traffic sound was as restful as the surf. Then I wondered if troopers actually slept there. I wasn't sure they did day-night shifts like the city fire department, but if they didn't sleep there why did they call it a barracks? I told you I had the fidgets.

There were only two people ahead of us at the testing-office counter. The room didn't seem as new as the outside of the building. It already had that ground-in dirtiness some kinds of public places get. Railroad waiting rooms were like that before the public discovered airplanes. I had never been to Imeson Airport so I didn't know if airports were like that too, but I wouldn't have been surprised. State unemployment offices are like that, both the one where you go to get your check, and the one where they list jobs.

The last person ahead of us was a skinny colored girl with braces on her teeth. She was getting her learner's permit. The guy behind the counter was trying to be just as hard on her as he could be. He looked bored, and that kind of person turns mean for the hell of it when they're bored. He finally marked a road sign wrong. Otherwise, he had to admit that her written test was perfect. He said it like she was sure to have cheated somehow. While he was typing up the permit some more colored people trooped in. They were all with the kid.

"I missed one," she told them. I thought she was going to cry.

"Ah thought you was gonna make uh purr-feck sko," the old woman said. She said it gentle, teasing.

"No'm, I guess not." She wasn't ready to be teased.

The fat guy behind the counter swapped her the permit for her money.   "It ain't no good until you sign it and you must carry it with you at all times," he said, just as nasty as he could. He was in a state uniform, but I don't believe he was a real road trooper. They never had many of that kind of road trooper in Florida even in the 1950s. I can't say about the rest of the South.

The whole bunch walked out with the girl and Corinne stepped up and announced she was here for the driving test. The tester was out and would be back. The clerk took down her name and we went back out in the clean sunshine to wait. The colored family was piling into a rump-sprung Rambler station wagon. The kid with the new permit was behind the wheel and took it out slow and careful, like she was patrolling enemy territory. Maybe she wasn't far wrong at that. The old woman was riding shotgun.

"Poor kid," Corinne said, surprising me. I mean she was from Georgia after all.

"Why?" I said.

"She really wanted to make a hundred, I bet."

"Sure. Wouldn't you?"

"I did."

"I guess that guy got his morning jollies out of not letting her have that one sign," I said.

"That's the way people like him always are," she said.

"That's why I memorized the whole book, in case they tried to say I missed one. They probably knew better than to try."

She was something, Corinne. "They probably did know better," I said.

A sleek new Ford coupe with the big round '59 tail lights came rumbling in and stopped. A guy with a ducktail haircut was driving, and a guy in a trooper Stetson sat beside him writing on a clipboard. They got out and came up the walk. The kid had his hands in his hip pockets and was trying not to swagger. After a while the guy in the Stetson came back.

"Mrs. Powell?" That was Corinne's second husband's name. The Burma veteran who had hair as blond as Little Luke's when he went away, and none at all when he came back.

I was thinking about all this stuff that I knew now about her life as she led him over to the Chev and he checked out the turn signals and all. For the first time she lost that Indian look and her face opened up a little. She was nervous, all right.

"Corinne?" I said.

"What?" She kind of bit it off, focused on the guy in the hat.

"Just make like he's got a Black Label in his hand instead of a clipboard. You'll be fine."

Chapter Eleven

There was a Krystal hamburger shop across the street and I walked over there to get a cup of coffee in a pasteboard cup and came back. I sat on the steps in front of the Highway Patrol barracks and looked at my watch. Corinne and the trooper had been gone ten minutes.

Sometimes they had pretty good coffee at the Krystal. This was one of the other times. The traffic went by on Riverside in a kind of moving traffic jam. I blew on the coffee and then sniffed it. For a minute I thought it sure smelled better than it tasted. A lot better. Then I smelled fresh roasted coffee all around me in the breeze off the St. Johns River. The smell was enough to perk you right up. It was coming from the Maxwell House plant down the river. Whenever they were roasting a batch, or whatever they did to release that aroma, the whole city seemed to smell like the best coffee you ever wanted to taste. It was my favorite thing about Jacksonville. I never had a day before to just sit doing nothing in the fall sun in Jacksonville and soak in that wonderful coffee smell and even the Krystal coffee couldn't spoil it for me.

For no reason at all, I suddenly wondered what Chris would be doing right now. Probably the same thing she had been doing when I was there last. I knew she had knitting classes or therapy or something, and visits by her doctors, but I had no idea what she really did except lay in that bed and watch TV. The sanatorium was set in a pretty campus of huge live oaks with Spanish moss draped all over them. There wasn't a palm tree over there. I had seen patients out walking and sitting on benches, even playing croquet, but never Chris.

I hadn't been over to see her for several weeks. I just kept putting it off. Sally's grandmother had called to say they hoped I could come for Thanksgiving. I told her I was pretty sure Dawson wouldn't let me off because of the big Georgia-Florida game in the Gator Bowl. The truth was I didn't want to go. If I didn't ask Dawson for Thanksgiving off until too late, he would just say no and I'd be off the hook. He didn't want a substitute cook messing with his Thanksgiving turkey dinners. I was trying to decide if I should feel bad about not wanting to go over there for Thanksgiving when the Chev came down Riverside.

They stopped where the beefed-up Ford had and sat there talking. I noticed that my stomach was tense and that surprised me. If Corinne got her license, would she still want to go riding with me? For some reason that was the first time I had thought about that specific question. Sure she would. She would want to practice now until she could afford to buy her car. She would feel like she had the right to drive now for sure. She was a big believer in your rights.

I wondered what kind of car she would buy. She would probably start driving it to work. Even at twenty-seven cents a gallon, it wouldn't take too much of her tip money to drive back and forth to work. I wondered if she might buy one of those little VW bugs that were starting to get so popular.

Volkswagen had just started that funny advertising campaign that year about small being better. Being small myself, I kind of appreciated that whole notion. As I recalled, the Beetles had a little four-speed gearshift on the floor. A real floor gearshift in miniature, like that one on Corinne's brother's truck up in Macon. More gears than the Chev even had, like she'd told me that night.

No matter what kind of car she bought, there would be no reason for us to go riding anymore. If we did go riding together after that, it wouldn't be the same thing that it had been up until now. It would be getting to be something else. It might be getting to be something else already, at least for me. Why does it always have to get to be something else with a woman you like? But it does, and you know it always does, unless you know when to quit. Well, it didn't have to get to be something else, did it? No, but it might. Well, let it get to be something else then and to hell with it.

They seemed to be staying in the car a long time. Maybe she had flunked. If she had flunked she would have to do a lot more driving to get over it. That would be okay with me because we could still go riding and it would still be okay. It would be fine. It would be the same thing as it had started to be, and wouldn't ever have to get to be anything else. Then later, if it did get to be something else, okay. I would be able to handle it then, if I just had a little more time for it to be the same as it had been. I haven't had much in my life that I really wanted badly, but all of a sudden I wanted that and I wanted it really badly. For her to have flunked so we could keep on going riding the way we had.

They finally got out of the Chev and as soon as she came around the car I knew she hadn't flunked. She wasn't looking like an Indian anymore. She was looking like a kid with a secret too big to hold inside. She looked fit to pop. Even the tester was grinning.

They came up. "Well?" I said.

She was almost hopping. "I did it! I did it! " She looked at the tester. "Didn't I?"

"You sure did, ma'am." He had a soft Florida drawl. He looked at me. "Your wife's a fine driver, Mr. Powell. She says you taught her. You did a fine job, sir, and I don't usually say that to husbands. She maxed the driving test."

My face must have got kind of funny looking, because

Corinne busted right out laughing with that big laugh of hers. The poor guy looked hurt.

"Uh," he said. "Uh, did I..."

"You're all right!" she said. "You are *all right!* No, sir, there's nothing wrong here at all. *Mr. Powell here* just didn't think I'd do that good. That's all. Let's go get my license."

They went in. I drank my coffee on down without tasting it. I don't know why his making a logical assumption like that got to me so bad. For some reason it made me feel guilty because I wasn't with Chris and didn't even want to be. I felt like an imposter about the tester's mistake. I felt half a dozen other things all at once that I couldn't put a name to except that they made me feel miserable and happy at the same time. It was like I was a teenager again. But it ached more because I wasn't.

The main thing was the way she had laughed at me, and not put the guy straight fast. The Corinne that I was used to was the one who put everything straight right off the bat. She didn't want anybody getting any wrong ideas about anything.

But now, this time, she hadn't done it. And she had laughed like crazy when she saw how her not doing it had crossed me up. I hadn't spoken up to correct him, because I was sure she would, in a heartbeat. But she hadn't, and I could see how she really got a kick out of how it had crossed me up. It looked like here came that something else, bigger than anything. I wasn't ready, but it looked like here it came, all right.

Chapter Twelve

I told Dawson I would take that next Tuesday the first week of November off instead of Thanksgiving, and drove over to Chris' folk's place as soon as I got off Monday night. I guess my conscience was bothering me. It always seemed to bother me worse when I was not really doing anything but wanted to do something real bad. The longer you don't do it, the worse you want to do it and the worse it bothers you that you want to. It gets to be like some kind of pressure in your head and starts squeezing.

Driving a long way is a good time for thinking about stuff like that. It never seems to get worked out in your mind when you're busy with everyday life but it all seems simple when you are driving somewhere. You always seem to forget it as soon as you get to where you're going, or I do. But at least you had it figured out for a while.

Sally was happy to wake up Tuesday morning and find me there. I was so glad to see her. I never had thought much about wanting children and neither had Chris, so Sally had just kind of happened to us, but I was glad she had.

I kept her out of school for the day, and we had a blast. That was a Beatnik word for having a good time that had just got popular, and we did. We had breakfast at a diner. She ate more strawberry waffles that I believed she could and didn't get sick from it either. We ordered her a bright blue fall coat at the Montgomery Ward catalog store in Lake City, delivery promised in a week as I recall.

Her grandmother fixed us a nice picnic lunch and we took a country drive to look at cattle and horses, and see if we could see an alligator in a creek. Sally missed seeing alligators and didn't understand why they wouldn't be in every little creek since we still lived in Florida. I told her if it snowed this winter she would know why, because alligators are allergic to snow. She gave me one of those looks the female species seem to have patented and told me that it was about as likely to snow in Lake City as we were to find an alligator this far north.

But we did see a whitetail doe running like the wind across a field. All the cows tried to run after her, clumsy and lead footed. Sally said it looked like they all wanted to be graceful as deer when they grew up, like the ugly ducking that became a swan.

"But since they're already grown they never are going to be deer are they?" She sounded very sad.

"If all the cows turned into deer where would we get milk?"

"Dad, you know I don't like milk!"

I felt stupid because I had forgotten. All I could think to say was that a lot of other kids did.

"Gramma tells me never to try to do something because other kids do it, Dad."

"Well she's right about that. Maybe she should tell the cows not to try to be deer, too."

That got her to giggling, and I was off the hook for a little while. Then she wanted to know if Mom was ever going to be healthy like the other moms she saw picking her friends up from school and whose houses Gramma let her visit. I said I hoped so. She wanted to know when. I said the doctors thought Chris could spend some short periods at home in the spring. I should have known better. She got real quiet and about to cry until I said we had time to go see the new Disney movie about Sleeping Beauty that was playing in Lake City before we went to see Mom that evening.

The sanatorium was harder to take than usual. Even

the lights in the hallway seemed dull. They seemed to draw all the oxygen out of the air. I never did like hospitals, the halls and the doors with people behind them, just lying there. They could have the measles or be dying and they all looked the same. The only time they looked nervous was when something changed in their routine. If there was a nurse in there with them, or a doctor, or visitors in their church clothes, the patients always looked as if the strain of bearing up was going to kill them. They called the one where Chris stayed a TB sanatorium, but the patients acted exactly like they did in hospitals.

Chris smiled at Sally once when we came in and then went on staring at the TV. It was one of those situation comedies with the dubbed-in laughter. They were big that year, thought not quite as big as Westerns. Christine had always hated situation comedies on the radio, long before there was TV, and she hated them worse on TV. She used to make a big thing about it when I wanted to watch *I Love Lucy* once in a while. Now she watched the television all the time regardless of what show was on. She just kept on watching almost like we weren't even there.

"What day is it?" she asked me.

"Tuesday."

She kept right on looking at the figures that jerked around on the screen, falling over things and pulling vaudeville faces.

"I didn't *think* it was Thanksgiving yet," she said. "I would have seen the Macy's Parade on TV." The thought that she might have missed the parade seemed to bother her.

"I see you got your hair trimmed," I said.

"Oh." She touched the clipped off curls where they lay against her neck. "It just kept on being hot," she said. "My neck kept sweating. Now it's too cold."

"It looks okay on you," I said.

"You like it long," she said.

"That looks fine, and it must be more comfortable."

"It is more comfortable anyway even now it's getting cold," she said.

"It looks fine."

"You said that."

"Yeah."

She kept right on looking at the television. I finally noticed the sound was turned too low to hear,

"You want me to turn the TV up?" I asked her.

"I'm not helpless."

"I know you're not. I just thought..."

"I've seen it already."

"Want me to turn it off then?"

"No!" She seemed vaguely alarmed at the thought.

"Change channels?"

"No. Just leave it alone!"

"Are you okay, Chris?"

"I'm okay. I'm just a little tired."

"Mom," Sally said, "Gramma said to tell you she's coming by tomorrow."

"Okay," Chris said. "You being good?"

"Her teacher says she's doing great according to your mother," I said.

"I know. The teacher came by to see me last week."

"Oh."

"I ain't got leprosy, you know."

"Mommy, what's leprosy?" Sally asked.

"It's a disease," I said.

"Does Mom have it? Does Mommy have leprosy?"

"No," I said. "Only niggers get it."

"Does Opal have it then?"

"Who's Opal?"

"She's Gramma's cleaning lady at home. What does leprosy do?"

"It makes people rot," I said.

"Oh, Walter for God's sake," Chris said. "See what you started?"

"Opal doesn't have it, Sally," I said.

Chris was watching the TV again like she didn't want any part of this. She was watching a *TIDE* commercial. The announcer looked like an idiot, mouthing his lines with the sound turned off.

"Chris?" I said.

"What?"

"I'm not going to be able to come over for Thanksgiving."

"Okay," she said.

"Daddy," Sally said, "how do you *know* Opal doesn't have leprosy?"

"It's the Georgia-Florida Bowl game," I said to Chris. "I have to work it. You know."

"Okay."

The comedy show was going off the air. Chris was watching the credits roll up the screen now.

"Daddy!"

I turned on her. "*What*, damn it?"

She pouted. "You don't have to yell! I just want to know how you can be sure Opal doesn't have it. *I* don't want to rot, and she irons all my clothes!"

"Opal can't catch it, and neither can you. Only niggers in Africa catch it."

"Darkest Africa, Daddy, like on the Jungle Jim Show?"

"Jesus Christ," Chris said to the television. A new show was coming on.

"That's it," I said. "Darkest Africa."

"Let's *go,* Daddy. Gramma said she'd wait supper!"

"Okay," I said. I gave her the car keys. "You can go open the car doors."

She went out of the room.

"Chris, I'll come over after Thanksgiving. I think Dawson is going to have to start closing at least a few more days. We're just not getting that much business."

"Okay." The new show was a Western. Chris had never liked Westerns, either.

"You never liked Westerns," I said.

"What else is there?" she said. "Shoot 'em up bang-bang." She looked at me and almost smiled. "Pernell Roberts is cute though."

"Who the hell is Pernell Roberts?"

"Adam on *Bonanza*. That new Western. You don't watch much TV huh?"

"We don't even have a television, Chris."

"We don't?" Her eyes shunted around like she was trapped. "I can't be where there's no TV, Walter. I'm no South African."

"I'm sorry I said that about Africa and leprosy," I said.

She lifted a hand and let it fall back. "I said leprosy first. I'm not talking about that. I guess if you don't watch television then you don't know that the South Africans won't let it in their country. A whole country without TV!" She was getting agitated."

"That won't happen here," I said. "Relax, Chris. I'll get a set when you're ready to come home."

"Color?" she said.

"What?"

"A color TV? Like Technicolor at the movies?"

I had no idea what something like that cost. "Sure," I said. "A Technicolor television."

She seemed to relax. "That'll be nice. We can watch my shows together."

For some reason her saying that made the walls seem to close in even worse than usual. I had to get out of there. "Want me to turn the TV up now?" I said.

"Okay," she said. She wasn't looking at me any more.

I went over and turned the volume up. "That about right?"

"That's fine."

"Guess I'd better be going. Take care of yourself."

"Okay." She was gazing at the television.

I went out. The cowboys and Indians were shooting hell out of each other on the TV. Shoot 'em up bang-bang.

Chapter Thirteen

I stayed over Tuesday night with Christine's folks and drove back early the next morning. My breath puffed out in front of me when I went out to crank the Chev, and I had to use the manual choke to smooth her out until she warmed up. On the highway I saw a couple of surplus Army jeeps with dog boxes for deer hounds mounted in back where the recoilless rifle or the Browning .50 used to go. The oak trees inland were shedding colored leaves and I stopped for gas in Olustee, where some hunters in straw cowboy hats were buying Nehis and Moon Pies. Their Ford pickup was full of lumber for building tree stands out in the flatwoods. Deer hunting in Florida was a lot different than in Ohio, but seeing the hunters out preparing, and the bright leaves, made me a little homesick for the autumns of my youth. It looked colder than it was and sure didn't resemble anything you'd see on a Florida Chamber of Commerce brochure. By the time I hit the coast it was mild enough to roll down my window.

I went through my apartment like a station break on the TV game of the week. I showered, shaved, got into fresh whites, grabbed up my dirty laundry and beat it. I dropped the stuff off at Cole's Cleaners.

Corinne was back in the kitchen picking up an order when I relieved the lunch cook. Just the sight of her now gave me a wallop. I had it bad all right, and all the trips in the world over to the sanatorium weren't going to cure it.

"Got you a car yet?" I said.

Her face immediately tightened into that Indian-head-on-a-nickel look. It was funny how her using that look on me could twist my insides. I was getting to have a pretty bad case of it all right. She took the order and started to walk out without speaking.

"Hey," I said, "this is me, remember? Walter the Driving Instructor."

"Big deal," she said.

She might as well have kicked me in the balls. I had it bad all right. But I tried one more time. "What's wrong? Did I do something?"

"Not you," she said. "*Him*."

"Him?"

"Daddy," she said, as if that explained everything.

"You mean Mr. Valland?"

"The son-of-a-bitch," she said. The absolute lack of expression in her voice made the words scary.

"Take it easy," I said. "Jesus, fish guts in the garbage can't smell *that* bad."

"He won't let me buy a car," she said.

That stopped me trying to be funny. "What do you mean, he won't *let* you? How can he stop you?"

"He can," she said. "Believe me, he can." She had never sounded completely defeated before and that was even scarier. "I gotta get this food out."

"But he can't just not let you buy a car! It's your money, ain't it?"

"That don't have anything to do with it."

"The hell it don't!"

"You don't know nothing about it. Not *nothing!*"

So there I was back outside again looking in. At least it wasn't me she was mad at.

"You're right," I said. "I just don't understand."

"What's to understand? The son-of-a-bitch, he just won't ever let us have any independence, not ever. He's just Mr. Big Shot, that's all. He ain't about to let us forget it. The bastard!"

She shut up and her face went right back into that

Valland death mask when she stalked out with the order. I wondered if it would change before she got to the paying customers.

It looked like it was going to be one of those long nights that come along, now and then.

Chapter Fourteen

We closed finally around midnight and I asked her if she wanted a lift home. She said she wasn't going home.

"Where you going, scooter-pooping?" I said. Scooter-pooping was a Georgianism I had picked up from her. It meant stepping out, partying, something like that.

"Maybe I am," she said. She was still tight and sullen.

"Want to go riding then?"

"I don't feel like driving tonight. It would just make me mad all over again."

"I'll drive then," I said.

She looked at me. "I thought you didn't like to just drive around."

"I don't like to drive around when I'm drinking beer. I'm not going to drink any beer tonight if you want to just ride around."

We were standing on the steps in front of the take-out door. There was nothing on in the restaurant but the night-lights, making strange patterns through the hanging kitchenware behind the takeout counter. Dawson and his wife were still in the office going over receipts, but you couldn't see those lights from here.

"Let's just go," I said.

"Okay," she said.

I unlocked the right-hand door and went around and started the car.

"Brr-r-r!" she said, hunching her arms across her breasts. I could see goose bumps on her forearms in the dash lights.

"It's getting to be winter, all right," I said. "Even in

Florida."

I left the choke knob halfway out and took a rag from the floor to wipe the dew off the rear window. Pretty soon it would be frost, even in Florida. The exhaust was puffing out whitely, and it tickled my ankles when I walked through it. The stars were sharp and clear and there was a new moon over the ocean that was just a sliver. I could even hear the surf thumping down on the beach. My blood was humming in my ears and I was excited as a teenager. I thought if the weather stayed like this it was going to be great football weather on Thanksgiving Day.

When I got back in the car, Corinne asked if I had antifreeze in the radiator. I said yes. Then she asked me if I had a heater, and I said yes.

"Does it work?" she said.

"Uh-huh."

"Want to turn it on just to be sure?"

I laughed, and she laughed. The cold seemed to have drained some of the tension out of her. I switched the heater on and she yelped.

"That air is *cold!*"

"Engine's just warming up. There, feel the change?"

I put the lights on, nudged the choke closed and dropped it into gear. The blower-air was losing its edge fast now.

"Ahh-h-h," she said. "Heat."

"Where to?"

"It don't matter. You decide." She slid down in the seat and propped her head back.

I went down First Street toward Ponte Vedra. We drove almost all the way to the Oasis without saying a word. I was beginning to think she had gone to sleep in the warmth from the heater. It was strange how completely different it seemed with me driving and her relaxing, with the heater on and the cold air slipping by the top of my head where I cracked my window to keep things from fogging up.

Finally I asked her if she was awake.

She sighed. "Yeah."

"Want to talk about it?"

"There's nothing to talk about."

"It might help to talk about it, though. You seemed so pissed earlier."

"Nothing will help except time." She straightened up. "We're almost to the Oasis."

"Want to keep going?"

"What do you mean?"

"We could drive down to St. Augustine, or over to the Orlando highway," I said. "There's an all-night truck stop over there on the Orlando road. I know the cook. He's almost as good as me. Or there's a bottle club in St. Augustine that serves pretty good steaks. We could go eat some steaks and dance a little maybe." My voice sounded funny in my own ears.

"Me in this?" She plucked at the front of the uniform.

"I don't care." Now my voice really sounded funny to me. She hadn't said no.

"I'm not going scooter-pooping in any greasy uniform. If I go out on the town with you, I'm going to dress up in style. Anyway, I'm not going out on the town."

"Why not?"

"Just turn around at the Oasis," she said. "He won't let me, that's why."

The Oasis still was jumping, to judge from the cars in the parking lot. I turned in and pulled over near the edge of the lot where the big barrier dunes started up and went all the way down to St. Augustine.

"You mean your daddy won't?"

"He won't let me do *anything*. I can't have any kind of a life of my own."

"What does Mrs. Valland say about all this?"

"Oh, *her*. Shit! She's afraid of him, always has been. He knows it too, don't think he don't. She's afraid he'll walk out on us. Run off with one of those slut-tramps that're always after him. She's not afraid he'll leave because he's got anything she needs, don't you go thinking that. That's been over a long time, ever since he fathered that little idiot bastard by that tramp in Macon. She's worried about my kids. Their daddys could get them away from me if he left. And old retired woman and a divorced waitress, not a proper home." I had never heard her sound so bitter. "That would kill her. Me, too, for that matter. But I ain't afraid of him!"

She paused for breath.

"What's all that got to do with you buying a car?" I asked her.

"I told you: he won't let me."

"It's still your money, ain't it? You must do all right in tips."

"I give my money to Mama and she pays for the kids' school stuff and gives the rest to him for the house. So no, it ain't mine, not really, none of it. Except I save out a little, and now I've saved up two hundred dollars. I could buy some kind of a car with that. Then maybe I could get a real job, maybe a federal one at one of these Navy bases. I've got government work experience from that arsenal in Macon. But if I did that, we would be out from under his thumb and he couldn't be the cock of the walk like he's been ever since my brothers went to war and then got married. Me and Mama could go anywhere we wanted in our own car and take the kids. But he says he's not going to buy another sack of groceries or anything else until I either give him that two hundred dollars to put in the bank, or give it to Mama to spend it on the house. Damn it, I don't want to!"

"Then it's simple," I said. "Buy you a car. I got a buddy who's a mechanic who can look at it for you and make sure it's in good running shape."

"I *can't,* don't you see that?" She was almost crying.

"Why?"

"Because he'd leave, all right, just out of pure meanness. Ben and Luther would be on us like a duck on a June bug to get their boys, before I could find a good job and get money coming in. The only way the court let me keep my boys in the first place is because I can provide them with a home. That's because of my parents."

"I don't get it. You're their mother."

"Ben and Luther both got married again. Both of them are war veterans. *Heroes.*" She sneered the word. "Luther's already been to court to try to get Little Luke once. He'd do anything to get his hands on him, but he can't, not legally, as long I'm living with Mama and Daddy and can provide what the court calls a proper home. It's been my sons' home long as they can remember. If Daddy moves out, that breaks it up and leaves a divorced waitress and an old lady who's never worked in her life, with both those *fine* married couples just waiting to get hold of Ben and Luke."

"Can they do things like that?"

"The courts can do any damn thing they want. That judge made it real plain he didn't like letting me keep them in the first place. But Daddy's real big in the Georgia Cracker party, so the judge didn't have any real choice. As soon as Daddy walks out that's over, and they swoop down on us like buzzards!"

I started the car and drove back north. Any thoughts I had about getting her off alone had been burned right out of my mind. No wonder she thought all men were shits. I had a notion she had sworn to God, or somebody, that no son-of-a-bitch was ever going to get her in the sack again, not ever. I thought I might have had a chance to talk her out of that, but as long as this was going on, there wasn't a snowball's chance in hell to use another of her favorite phrases.

Her opening up like that about her troubles let me know how far I really was from ever getting to first base with her. Right now that didn't matter. Later it would, but not now.

Now I was just sick to think of a man who would hold something like that over his own daughter. It made me mad, too. I wondered how tough Mr. Bull Valland would be if I took my Solingen chef blade and opened him up like a hog for a Georgia barbecue without cutting his throat first. Right then I was so mad I knew I could do it. Or I could fillet him like one of his red snappers and not even regret it when they marched me off.

But I knew doing something like that would probably just get Ben and Luke taken away all the faster to save them from the uproar and the publicity. I was so clear about how that would be, it was like I really was going to go get my knives and that was the only thing that stopped me. I was thinking about it so hard that I almost forgot Corinne was there. When we got back up close to Dawson's, she suddenly let out a sound like she was strangling.

"Stop!" she said.

I had never heard fear in her voice, but I heard it then.

I slammed on the brakes so hard she almost banged her head on the windshield.

"What in hell--?"

"Look! "

I looked where she was pointing, up toward Dawson's. A dark car eased out of the parking lot and turned north. It wasn't Dawson's new Cadillac. It only had one dim taillight. It was a high-wheeled old car that sat tall on seventeen-inch rims, something pre-war, built when they still made running boards. Like maybe a 1937 Plymouth with a floor-mounted gearshift.

"Oh, Jesus Christ," Corinne said, like she was praying or something.

"What is it? What's wrong?" Her being scared was contagious.

"It's Daddy," she said. "Don't keep driving north behind him or he'll see us. He's got eyes like a hawk."

My internal organs seemed to knot all up and squeeze up behind my breastbone. I made a jerky left turn inland. She watched the single taillight out of sight like she was hypnotized.

"What would he be doing at Dawson's this time of night?" I said.

"Coming to get me."

"When's he ever done that before?"

"He hasn't! But Rennie's been running his mouth off about you and me." It was the first time she ever had mentioned Rennie since I asked her about him going fishing with her father that day. Now I really was scared. Why hadn't she told me this before?

"Daddy decided that the whole argument over my car money was your fault about me getting a driver's license. That if he wanted me to have a driver's license he would have got me one.'

"That's stupid! But what's that got to do with Rennie?"

"Rennie's been making up stuff about you and me. Remember you said nobody believed you were just teaching me to drive? Well Rennie told that to Daddy, that nobody on the whole Beaches believed it, and everybody was laughing at him behind his back. Rennie even had the nerve to say--to--" She spluttered to a stop, breathing hard.

"He thinks we've been messing around?" I said. I turned back south on Penman road.

"We had an awful fuss last night about me riding with you any more, and about me getting a car. I said I was sick and tired of walking. Daddy said all right then, he would come and get me from now on. I never thought he'd do it, though, and miss the Late Show on TV."

"Well, it looks like he came down here tonight, all right."

"Rennie just started this to cause trouble because I wouldn't screw him. He knows Daddy's as bad as them old mountain men on *Gunsmoke* about his womenfolk. Don't want us even talking to other men."

It was the first time she'd come right out and said Rennie tried to get her in bed. I just kept on driving and looking for high-wheeled black cars hiding up side streets. I couldn't think what else to do.

"Walter?" she said. "I'm sorry. I'm really sorry I got you into all this, just because you were trying to be a nice guy. I haven't had much to do with nice guys. I'll take a taxi home from now on. Daddy can't argue about me using my own money for that."

"You don't have to spend it all like that," I said.

"Yes I do, until this all dies down. I don't want you getting hurt on account of me."

"If you want to take a cab, you take a cab." My throat was tight and I had to force the words out. "Just as long as you know you don't have to. As long as you know you got a ride from me whenever you want it." I stopped, and then forced the rest of it out. "Anywhere you want to go, too. You hear me?"

"I better go home now, Walter. They'll be in a hell of a fuss by the time I get there, and I'm just so damn tired."

"You want me to drive you?" We were back out on Beach Boulevard going toward the Inland Waterway bridge.

"I better take a cab."

"Okay," I said. "Okay, I'll drive you over to the taxi company. You'll get one faster from there."

Chapter Fifteen

The morning after I dropped Corinne off at the taxi company on Jacksonville Beach I woke up before Mabel called me. First time I had done that in a long time. It was around nine or ten in the morning. The sun was slanting through the Venetian blinds and the room was full of dust motes hanging like specks of gold in the stripes of sunlight. It still felt cold from the nighttime. I was going to have to think about coal oil for the heater before too long.

I had a bad taste in my throat. My bladder acted like it was about to spring a leak. I remember that seemed odd because I hadn't had any beer the night before.

I emptied my bladder and shaved, brushed my teeth and burned out that bad taste with Listerine. By then I had a headache. I took a couple of aspirin and went back to bed and died for about an hour. A twisted kind of dream woke me up. Corinne was in it, and a big old pre-war Packard like in gangster movies. Not Bull Valland himself, or his '37 Plymouth, just the Packard, dark and dangerous as a U-boat in the night.

I woke up the second time scared, the way you do sometimes. The dust motes were still there, glittering in the sunlight. I lay there a long time until my heart slowed down. But my brain didn't.

I wondered if Corinne would be at work today. Sure she would. But she might not. She might not want to work there anymore. Bull Valland might make her quit to put more pressure on her to turn loose of her car money. Even if he let her keep working at Dawson's, he would for sure tell her not to have anything to do with me. I had given up trying to pretend that her being thirty years old and divorced twice had anything to do with what Bull Valland could force her to do. He could make her do anything he wanted her to do, holding her kids over her head.

If Bull told her she could keep working but not to have anything to do with me, she would try to do it. I bet that's what he would tell her to do, all right. It's the kind of thing a man like him probably would do.

But you can't just go right on working with somebody like nothing has happened when things change between you. Because as soon as somebody isn't speaking to somebody else at work, everybody knows it. I've seen it too many times. Then everybody at work wants to know why they're not speaking. If the one who suddenly isn't speaking won't say why, they start in on the one who is not being spoken to. They ask the one not being spoken to anyway, just to compare what each of them says. I used to think people who worked in restaurants must not have much of a life to be so vitally interested in every little detail of everybody else's.

The waitresses would all talk to each other about Corinne not speaking to me. They would say they were doing it to warn everybody not to put Corinne or me in a situation where we would be expected to talk to each other, to keep things from being awkward. But boy would they be loving the gossip and the suspense of it. There would get to be little strained pauses in the daily grind of the job once everybody knew our business, everybody waiting to see what else might happen next.

Things would keep on that way and if some kind of understanding wasn't reached pretty quick, one or the other of the two who weren't talking anymore was going to get fired. Some bosses fired both to make a lesson of both parties, and to try to keep anybody else from starting in on some kind of personal thing at work. Dawson might do that if he had another head cook on tap but I didn't think he did.

Any work two people do under the same roof is just too close for anything like not speaking to each other to go on for very long. All the bosses I ever had knew that and tried to keep personal relationships on the job from happening, but they kept right on happening anyway. I had never thought something like that would happen to me though.

Over my years in the business I had seen only two people trying to back out of an honest-to-God affair who managed to take it back to the way it was before they were an item. We all worked the night shift at a Pennsylvania Turnpike truck stop east of the Alleghenies the year after Roosevelt died. They were the only two I ever saw who made it work. It seemed phony and strained for a while but sometimes they could pull it off. Both of them worked at it and that made things seem normal enough so that nobody else was uncomfortable and nobody had to be fired. One of them left in due course of time anyway and that was that. I had always admired their style.

All the other similar situations that I remembered had been real affairs that went sour for various reasons and ended up with somebody getting fired. This between Corinne and me was too different for me to have any idea about how it would work out.

She would be on orders from headquarters, and not even from a husband. She never seemed like the kind to take orders from anybody. But the way she told it she had no choice because of the kids. So I had to somehow figure out how to deal with it.

Deal with what, people might ask me if they knew that nothing had gone on between us. What the hell did people know anyway? I had to deal with it all right. That morning it seemed liked the hands on my clock by the bed were never going to move.

Waking up early had been strange enough, and then the bad dream. But time slowing down like that after I woke up the second time was just too much. I began to realize that I just had to know what had happened when Corinne got home last night. Was Bull waiting? Did they have an argument? Maybe he had beat her up. Maybe he still treated her like a child that he could take a strap too. Just thinking that made me feel weak and sick.

The hands on clock wouldn't move. Two p.m. at Dawson's would be too late to find out what happened to her. Too late for what I didn't know. Just too late.

Some kind of bile from my stomach had worked up in my throat and it had that awful taste again. Probably because I hadn't eaten anything since dinner the night before. Maybe I was getting an ulcer. I tried to swallow and had a hard time. My mouth was dry. Parched is more like it.

I could call her. I could call her and find out if she was okay.

I had never called her before or even thought about calling her. I sure couldn't just go over there. No way. It wasn't my business. The idea of calling her scared me almost as bad as the dream about the Packard.

I forced myself to lie there looking at the sunlight reflected on the ceiling and try to go back to sleep. I had always been able to go back to sleep if I woke up early after a night shift, which I almost never did anyway. It had always seemed easier for me to sleep in the daytime than at night. It didn't seem easier that morning. My throat got tighter and my mouth got drier and suddenly my pulse was beating again like I had just run up some stairs. When I rolled on my side, the pillow was full of the thump of blood in my ears. My ears felt hot. I ignored it and ignored it and finally it slowed down. I almost dozed.

I don't even know her phone number, I thought. I could find out easy enough. Maybe the phone number wasn't listed though. Maybe they didn't even have a phone. Lots of people didn't then on the Beaches. Why should the Vallands have one? They were new on the Beaches, and didn't have anybody much to call. All their real friends were still in Georgia and the other kind too.

She had told me about the other kind of friends, who would invite themselves down to Florida for a vacation at the Beaches now that they knew somebody who lived three doors from the ocean. Bull liked to play host to people he had known up there in politics. The family wound up sleeping on rollaway beds in the hot interior of the house, giving up their breezy porch beds for Georgia guests who tracked beach sand over the floors and left it to clog the bathroom drains. That outside shower I'd seen in their yard was Bull's one concession after Mrs. Valland had nagged and nagged about the sand and about playing motel maid to people she hardly knew.

Thinking about all that was, I guess, a way of passing time and trying to keep from thinking about calling her. Not having a phone would discourage a lot of the freeloaders who might call up looking for directions to the beach house. The Vallands probably didn't have a phone just because of that. Corinne said even Bull was getting tired of it. So not having a phone would cut down a lot of unexpected visits. I made a bet with myself they didn't have a phone number. Then I thought it was silly to lay in bed wondering. So I looked in the phone book. All that complicated thinking just to trick myself into looking in the phone book for their number.

They were in there all right. There was only half a pages of Vs, and only one Valland, Leonard A. (Bull), CHerry 3-4081. It didn't say Bull in the phone book, but I wondered if even his mother had called him Leonard. I had eaten hamburgers with the Leonard A. Valland family of Jacksonville Beach. There was nothing in the world wrong with my giving them a call.

Mrs. Valland answered on the third ring.

"This is Walter, from the restaurant," I said. "The man who ate your hamburgers and drank your tea."

"Oh, yes," she said in that soft drawl. "How are you this morning?"

"All right. Say, could I speak to Corinne?"

"I'm sorry, she's still asleep."

"Oh," I said. I hadn't counted on anything as ordinary as that. I should still be asleep too.

"She got in late last night. She said you had to work later than usual getting ready for Thanksgiving."

So she was telling lies at home now. Brother.

"Walter? I imagine you were at the restaurant late, too, since you're the head cook."

"Yeah," I said. "Yeah, the head cook works if anybody works. Uh, she didn't seem to be feeling very well when we got off work. She's all right, isn't she?"

"Oh, yes. She's just tired, needs her sleep. She'll have to be careful, though, the winter is coming on, and it's colder than we expected it to be down here in Florida."

"It was pretty chilly last night all right. Well, I'm glad it was nothing serious. I guess I'll see her at work then?"

"Probably you will. Thank you for calling, Walter, that was nice of you."

"Thank you," I said. "Say hello to the boys and to Mr. Valland, will you?"

There was a brief pause. Then, "...yes, of course. All right. Good bye, Walter."

"Is something wrong?"

"No, nothing. Bye, now."

I hung up and stared at the dust motes in the sun. I

was remembering how pleasant it had been to sit in their backyard that Saturday until Bull came home. Now there was that hesitation in Mrs. Valland's voice, and I wasn't just imagining it. Her last words had come out awkwardly. I wasn't Walter the nice man teaching her daughter to drive anymore. I was Walter the problem.

I did manage to doze off after that, and dreamed I was dying of thirst. Mrs. Valland was pouring a pitcher of iced tea over me, and I could feel the cold on my chest but couldn't open my mouth to taste it. The phone jerked me out of it. My first hope was that it was Corinne calling me back, but I knew it wasn't, and I was right. It was Mabel.

Chapter Sixteen

Corinne was at work, all right. She was in the kitchen drinking coffee when I got there, and looking at the afternoon newspaper.

"Hi." she said.

"Hello yourself. You're early today."

"It was just making me sick staying around home listening to that. Another minute of it and I would of got sick. I swear I would have."

"There wasn't any trouble was there? I was afraid there was going to be trouble," I said.

"Mama said you called."

I was embarrassed about it now. I was wide awake, it was broad daylight and the busboys were slamming dishes in the dishwasher, talking a mile a minute about something or other. Calling her seemed pretty silly right now.

"I shouldn't have called," I said. "If he's acting like that about the car money, then me calling might just make it worse."

"You're catching onto him pretty quick, aren't you? That's why I came in early today. He just kept on and on about that until I was sure I was going to get sick."

"About the car money?"

She nodded. "And about you calling today. And about all the rest of it, us going riding at night and stuff. That marshal, Billy Jarvis, and that man at the liquor store ain't the only ones who can jump to a conclusion."

I didn't say anything. I couldn't. I was thinking here we go for sure now, I'm going to get the hell beat out of me for something I never even had the pleasure of doing. I wondered if Bull would kill me or just mess me up like he had Bill Ombear. I couldn't seem to really worry about it just then, I just kind of wondered. Bull couldn't really be going to come after me. He probably was, though.

"What's wrong with you?" Corinne said.

"What do you mean?"

"You look sick yourself."

"I'm scared," I said.

"Of Daddy?" Her lip curled.

"Scared to death."

"No you ain't, or you wouldn't have called me up. You ain't scared, you're just pretending."

"I'm doing a good enough job of pretending to convince me," I said.

"You ain't though."

"God damn it, what do you know about it?"

"You called me up, that's what I know about it. Ever since he beat up that chickenshit Ombear, people have been walking around like he was God almighty."

"Ombear is pretty tough," I said.

"*Him?* Shit, *I* could have whipped him. Didn't I ever tell you they called me Jack Dempsey when I was a kid? Ombear wasn't nothing as tough as Harvey."

"Harvey?"

Her face had that Indian look again. "Harvey worked with me up at the arsenal before we came to Florida. He was a supervisor. He got the job because of veteran's preference, wounded in action in the Pacific, rotated home. He had a bunch of them medals like Bob Lee won in the war. Bob Lee said Harvey's was real ones, too, as good as his, even if Harvey was a Marine. Bob Lee was in the Army. We don't think much of Marines."

"Bob Lee? Harvey? Was Harvey your second husband? You're losing me fast."

"Bob Lee is my brother. No, I wasn't never married to

Harvey. Harvey was a gun sergeant in the Marines, Bob Lee said. I guess I thought all sergeants had guns, though."

"Gunnery sergeant probably," I said. "That's a Marine rank."

"He was okay for the only Marine I ever met," she said. "I hate the God damn Marines. They torture those poor boys awful up there at that Paris Island training place in South Carolina. I read about all that in the newspapers. I already told Ben and Little Luke I'd kill them if they tried to join the Marines. Ben sure liked Harvey. Harvey came around a few times. Then we found out he was married. Daddy threatened to break his neck."

"And then Bull broke his neck," I said. "This is beginning to sound like summer reruns on TV."

"No, he didn't break Harvey's neck, smart aleck. You're awful smart alecky for somebody who's half scared to death."

"I always get that way when I'm scared," I said. "Okay, what happened?"

"Well, Harvey got real loud and said he just loved to play pattycake with loud-mouthed crackers, and he'd just toss Daddy around with that Jewjitsy stuff. You know, that special Jew fighting they teach Marines how to do."

"Oh-ho," I said. "So what happened?"

"Well, he tried to flip Daddy. But Daddy wouldn't flip. Daddy picked Harvey up and threw him through the screen door. Then he went out on the porch and picked him up again and threw off the porch. He broke Mama's rose trestle."

"Who did? Harvey?"

"When he landed. Then he got up and ran across the street and locked himself in the men's bathroom at the gas station over there. Daddy grabbed a tire iron and tried to beat the door down. Three of the fellers over there tried to stop Daddy and get him to calm down. He broke one of their arms and another one's nose before they did get him calmed down. He kept yelling he'd show that married bastard how to fight a Jew. Harvey got away while they were holding onto Daddy. You should have seen him running down Central. Harvey was an excellent runner." She half smiled.

"Did Harvey have Bull arrested for assault?" I asked her.

"Are you kidding? Daddy would have killed him for sure, then. Besides, Daddy knows everybody up there in the Cracker party. They would have run Harvey out of town, but he left anyway. He had done left his wife and kids before he started coming around to see me, and he just took off for good."

"What about the gas station guys?"

"They apologized for interfering, and Daddy said it was okay, no hard feelings" she said. "Daddy drove the one with the busted arm to the hospital."

"Did he pay the doctor bill?"

"Why? That guy knew better than to try to hit him with a two-by-four. He was lucky Daddy only broke his arm."

"These Beaches ain't Bull Valland's town, though," I said.

"Then what did they do to him about Ombear?"

She had me there. "Nothing, the way I hear it."

"That's what they'll probably do to him if he hurts you, too. Nothing."

"I wish you wouldn't talk about my funeral before I buy the ground," I said.

She grinned. "See? I knew you weren't all that afraid!"

"I'm so scared my knees feel weak just thinking about it," I said.

"Bullshit. You can't fool me. You're little, but you're feisty. I can tell."

I wanted to feel good about her talking to me like that, but I felt like a phony. I just shook my head. "I wish *I* could tell," I said. "I'm afraid I'll shit my pants if he comes close to me."

She busted out with that big laugh of hers. "You know what? You're a born comedian. You really are."

"Glad you think so. We better quit yakking and get to work, though."

She nodded, put down the cup and sailed out toward the porch, still grinning.

I drank some coffee myself. If she kept on talking like that she would have me believing I wasn't scared of Bull. It had been so long since I wasn't afraid of something that I couldn't really remember what it felt like to not be afraid. It did seem like Bull Valland was an unreasonable amount to start not being afraid of, all at once. I didn't say that to her, though. After my strange sleepless morning, her smiling at me like that made me feel too good.

Chapter Seventeen

Corinne took a taxi home that night and the next night, Friday. We didn't have much of a chance to talk, but at least we were still talking, and the way she had joked with me and smiled at me had me feeling pretty good about things. The good feeling lasted until I got over to Bennett's Motel Friday night to play poker as usual and there was Rennie Cross, drinking a beer and watching the play.

It wasn't like it was unusual for Rennie to be there, but he hadn't been a regular for a while now, not since I had learned about him and Ombear getting beat up by Bull Valland. Somehow the minute I walked in the door I knew he was there to start in on me. I don't know how I knew, maybe just the way his eyes lighted up when I came in.

I played it straight up and hoped that I was wrong, that Rennie would stay out of my business. I said hello to the regulars and nodded to Rennie and went back to the bathroom. They always dumped a couple of big sacks of crushed ice in the tub and shoved the longneck bottles of beer way down it. The bottles would get really cold and beaded all over with moisture and almost frosted. The boys did that summer or winter. I picked up one, tossed a half-dollar in cup and popped the bottle cap off on the Coca-Cola opener screwed to the wall.

"Hiya, Walter," Rennie said when I came back out. The way he said it made my stomach crawl. Here it came, all right.

"What's up?" I said, keeping it neutral.

"Nothing much," he said, grinning real big and silly.

He nudged an elbow into Jimmy Shattuck's ribs and winked. Shattuck was a big dumb cab driver that Rennie buddied around with when he wasn't running with Ombear's crowd. Shattuck was grinning at me too. Then Shattuck laughed right out loud.

"Is that right, Walter?" Shattuck said. "Is that right, you got nothing up? And I do mean--up."

"I don't know," I said, still hoping to get past this. "I guess it depends on what you're talking about."

I could feel the skin on my skull drawing up tight the way those goatskin drums down in the Bahamas shrink when the Goombay bands heat them over a slow fire. I don't know why I thought of that, except my skull felt the way the goat would feel if he was still inside the skin when they heated it and stretched it on the drum. My eyes felt like they were popping right out of my head.

Shattuck just kept on chuckling, huh-huh-huh, like he was retarded or something. "Hell, you know what I'm talking about," he said, real smiley friendly like. "If something was up before, it sure isn't going to get up now, is it? Ask me how I know, why don't you, Walter?"

I just stood there, not saying anything now, holding my bottle of beer. That bottle had been ice cold to start with, but it had begun to feel warm in my hand already.

"Now, now," Rennie said. "Now, now, Jimmy." He was almost clucking like a hen. "You can't expect an answer from a man whose jaws are so tight he can't even speak. Can you?"

"I guess not," the cab driver said. "No, you're right. I guess you can't." He kept up that steady chuckle between words.

"I guess I'll have to answer for Walter," Rennie said. "No, there's nothing going to be getting up for poor old Walter now, because she is being a good little girl now like pappa told her and getting that sweet little pussy home in a cab as soon as Dawson's closes."

So here it was, out in the open.

"You stop," I said. My voice cracked in the middle.

They both laughed even harder then, holding onto each other. They were a good bit drunk already. The players around the card table were trying to finish out their hand of five-card stud and hear everything that was being said at the same time. Then the hand was over and they just sat there watching us out of the corners of their eyes. One of them was shuffling, but his heart wasn't in it and he didn't look about to deal just yet. Nobody was going to interfere, that was easy to see.

The center of the room seemed lit up funny, like a prizefight arena. It was so bright, and I could see every detail so clearly, but at the same time it was dull and kind of blurry around the edges. Rennie Cross and Shattuck sounded like they were off across there somewhere laughing down a culvert at me.

"It was a sweet pussy while it lasted, though, right?" Rennie said.

"You stop," I said again. I whispered, rather. My throat was tight and dry.

Their words seemed to come in like ocean waves when you are underwater in the surf, rushing over the top of you before you're ready, hissing, lifting you, trying to pull you up to the surface—and then gone on past to the beach, leaving you in the slack water exhausted from fighting to stay down and hold your breath at the same time.

"Well, she was sweet, wasn't she?" Shattuck said. "Wasn't she, Walter? You can tell us, we're your buddies, and you got more of that sweet pussy than anybody on the Beaches, give you that at least, you little shit. Who would have thought it? Was she tight, real tight, one of those second hand virgins, or was she one of those big juicy ones you could drop an ice cream churn down?"

"You shit," I said. "You lousy shits. You shut up."

Rennie stopped laughing. "What did you call us,

Walter?"

Their kind always gives you that one last chance to crawl. I've crawled before to people like them after my mouth overloaded my ass, ashamed as hell, but did it to get away without a beating.

"I called you a shit," I said. My voice was stronger now. "You horseshit, you."

"Don't start getting tough, Walter," Jimmy Shattuck said. He wasn't laughing now, either.

"You're just as much a shit as he is, you lousy fat tub of shit."

"Now that's enough!" Shattuck said.

"That's not even nearly enough, you tub of shit. You sorry sack of shit."

Now I was past the chance to crawl and I was okay. I couldn't get out of it now, and didn't want to. They would be very self-righteous in their anger at what I called them when they were just having fun, and nothing would stop whatever happened now.

"You better shut up now," Rennie said, mean-quiet. "Fun's over now, Walter. You better shut up now."

"Or what, you lousy shit?"

"You better not say another word if you know what's good for you," Shattuck said.

"You know what you can do," I said. Then I told him.

"Now that's going too far, Walter. You better stop, right this minute!"

"And break it off in there, you shit! Break it off right up to there."

Shattuck hit me, right out of nowhere. I never saw it come. I never even felt it. There was no pain or anything like that. Just a sudden change in everything and I was flat on my back on the floor. I never felt myself fall. I was just on the floor without knowing how I got there and the room lights were way up there over me, as far away as the sun. I could hear laughter again, way up there in the lights. When I tried to get up they laughed harder.

A shadow crossed my vision and I heard Shattuck say, "How do you like it now, you prissy little shit. There's plenty more where that came from."

I was on my feet now. I still had the bottle in my hand. It hadn't even broken, just spilled beer all over me. The bottle was slippery, and I was having trouble seeing.

"Want some more?" I heard Shattuck say.

I looked toward his voice. Something like a bomb went off on the side of my head. My knees just caved in, and I went down like a pile of soggy straw.

This time I was on my face and this time the voices in the room were just a rumble, far off, like cars on the old covered bridge in Ohio where I used to fish when I was a kid. The little creek under the bridge would run full and muddy every time it rained, and then low and clear on bright summer days after the winter snow and the messy springs. It would run clear and cold around exposed damp gravel bars that crunched and slid under your bare feet so that you sunk in when you walked, cold and gritty.

I went far into myself then, like a dream kind of. I saw the little smallmouth bass I used to catch in the creek before Ma died that last bad winter. I could feel the water on my numb bare feet and how cold the water was when I filled my old sailor hat and put it over my sunburned head, turning warm as it tricked down through my hair and clothes. The memory was so pure and clear I thought for a minute I had been killed. This was Ma's Heaven she always talked about where whatever made you happy was there. Ma said it was all so pretty in Heaven and we would all end up together and be happy forever. I felt like crying I was so happy that everything she told me had all been true.

Then Shattuck slapped me out of it, hard, hurtingly,

hurting badly now, one-two, one-two, back and forth. It was blood not warm creek water on my face.

I was back on my feet somehow and the room was unreal after where I had come back from. It was bright like a circus tent with the show over and the crowds all gone except for that dim circle of poker players, frozen, not moving, not alive.

Then I felt the beer bottle still in my hand, broken now, the long neck solid and unslipping in my hand, the other end almost weightless where the heft of the beer had been. I threw the bottle into Shattuck with everything I had, all my weight behind it. I felt its edges catch in him before the fear came sweeping up from his belly and weakened his arms where he tried to hold me.

Shattuck let me go and pulled back. I was alone, still holding the bottle, both of them in front of me now. Their faces were suddenly pale and afraid, their eyes dark holes. A sliver of glass glittered like a jewel above Shattuck's belt buckle right in the bulge of his belly. The brown glass was smeared bright red, mine or his I didn't know, and there was a wet stain down the front of his pants. I didn't know if he was bleeding or had wet himself.

Rennie was licking his lips. "Now, Walter, take it easy."

"Did you hit me too?"

"Now, Walter..."

"*Did you?*"

He licked his lips again. "I--no. No. That was just Jimmy."

"You bastard!" Shattuck said at him out of the side of his mouth. He couldn't take his eyes off the bottle's edges, jagged and red-smeared in my hand.

"Jeez," said Rennie. "Jeez, Walter, you must have fell on that bottle to break it like that. You must be cut bad. You better let me..."

"I'll let you eat this goddamn bottle if you want to," I said. "I'll do that for you, you lousy shit. Oh, you lousy shit." I was holding onto myself very tightly. I had never held on to anything so tightly as I was holding myself just then.

"Now, look, Walter," Shattuck said. One hand was pressing his belly and the other was out toward me, like asking for a handout.

"Just shut up," I said. "You just shut up. I'm going out of here now. I'm going to go get in my car and leave. If you don't want to eat this, then get away from that god-damned door!"

"But hell, Walter," Rennie said. "You're cut. We ought to..."

"*Move!*"

They moved, and I went by them as fast as I could, sideways. If they had only known it, they could have breathed on me and blown me right over. Maybe they knew. They could have known. They could have known it and been afraid to try it, too. Maybe they thought they would kill me if they tried it. Or maybe they actually were afraid of me. Maybe they thought I could cut them so bad they would bleed to death before anybody could stop it. Oh god how I would have tried, and I guess they knew that now. Anyway, they didn't try, and then I was out the door into the cold air.

"I'm going to my car," I said. "You try to come out here before I leave and I'll blow your god damn brains out. You hear me? I may blow your god damn brains out anyway."

They looked at each other and back at me through the door.

"You got a gun, Walter?" Rennie said.

"Come out and see." I slammed the door and tried to run to the Chev. I dropped the bottle and heard it smack and shatter on the paving. I was half in the car when the motel door opened and spilled light outside.

"Come out," I yelled. "Come on out, by god, and stand in the light like that, you stupid bastards!"

They slammed the door shut fast. I got the Chev started with the manual choke all the way out and slammed out of there. I drove three of four blocks by sheer instinct before the fuel mixture stalled me. I coasted over on the wrong side of the street and leaned out and puked my guts out. It came out hot and smoking in the cold. By the time I could focus again and close the choke, the Chev was ready to go again

I thought I'd croak if I didn't get my mouth washed out and some water in me. The back of my throat tasted like a lost weekend. My right ribs had a spot that was stinging the way a cut does when it begins to hurt. The bottle had cut me all right. Maybe badly. I was shaking like coming down off a bad drunk, but at least I could see a little now. I don't remember exactly how I got home.

Chapter Eighteen

My hands were shaking so bad I had a hell of a time getting the apartment door open. After I got my mouth washed out with Listerine and my shoes off and into bed, I couldn't get warm. My teeth chattered so bad I was afraid they might crack. I crawled out of bed and got one of my mother's heavy old quilts I'd had all my life, and a bedspread. The extra weight of the covers pressing down on me seemed to steady me a little. After a while my teeth stopped chattering.

I still had on my clothes. The kitchen smell on my clothes made me sick. The inside of my mouth was cut where Shattuck had slapped me, and was stinging now. I kept thinking that all that just couldn't have happened to me. It couldn't have happened but it had. I had tried to ram that broken bottle all the way through that bastard Shattuck and might have, if I had a better grip on it. I wished I had. No, I didn't. I just wished none of it had ever happened.

I was weak and sick all over. Not throwing-up sick. I had got that out of the way at least. Just sick. I kept shivering for a while and finally stopped. It was getting good and warm under the extra covers now. I started dozing in fits and starts. I wanted to get up and get my clothes off and go to bed right, but I couldn't. It was too warm under the covers now to lose the warmth by getting up again. Even the kitchen smell didn't seem so bad anymore.

I was warm and didn't have to think about anything now. I didn't have to remember anything or think about how I was going to face the world tomorrow. I didn't even have to think about Corinne. Right now, all I wanted was not to have to think about anything, anything at all.

When I woke up the next time I was wide-awake and there was a stinging, rubbing ache in my side where I was lying on it. I had been cut all right, and now the dull misery of it was setting in. I rolled over to try to ease it, and somebody spoke out loud in my room.

"You awake, Walter?"

I nearly jumped out of my skin. This is just a saying until you get scared so bad you really try to do it. Or at least it seems like you do. Then you know where a saying like that comes from and I really knew right then, all right.

I was afraid to move. I was paralyzed. I was so scared my heart almost stopped beating. I couldn't even breathe. I had my mouth wide open to breathe and I just couldn't. I tried to make believe there was nobody really in my room. I was just dreaming it. I would *not* look around to see who it was. See who? There was nobody there. If there was, and if I saw him, I was done for.

It was like when you're a kid and they turn the lights out and things creep up on you. I used to think if those things in the dark didn't know that I knew they were there, they wouldn't bother me. You had to pretend very hard that you didn't know they were there. You make believe those shadows are just chairs and clothes hanging up and things like that, not something that will get you for sure if they know that you know they're there.

I suddenly realized that must be why I liked night shifts, so I could sleep in the daytime when it was safe. What a stupid reason for a grown man.

"Walter?"

I didn't move a muscle. If I moved, it would pounce me in the heavy bedcovers and kill me dead without a chance. He would stab through the bedcovers and through me, and I would sting and rub all over, and...

"Walter, it's me, Billy, Walter. Are you awake?"

When he said it, I think I nearly passed out from the shock of it being just Billy Jarvis and not those dark things from childhood that almost did me in.

It could have been Rennie or Shattuck, too, coming after me to get even about that broken bottle and I would have been a dead duck. Now was a hell of a time to remember to lock my door. Now was way too late to think about that real grown-up reason to be scared. But this time I didn't have to get grown-up scared, because it was just the town marshal.

A big dog growled in the room and my overhead light came on. That dog scared the sleep right out of me. That growl almost scared the shit loose, too. It was my night for being scared. I popped up like a jack-in-the box, covers or no covers.

Billy said, "Easy, Walter." Him and his Great Dane were standing by my bedroom door. I couldn't see them but as blurs.

"What do you want?" I said.

"I just dropped by to see if you're all right."

The dog growled again. He didn't like the tone of my voice to his master. Great Danes are supposed to be friendly, and Billy's always had been friendly to me, but he was at work now.

"Get that god-damned horse out of here," I said.

"Now don't be that way, Walter."

"Just take him out of here."

"Now, look. I just came by because they said you might need some doctorin'." He waved a big tin box in his left hand. It was the size of a briefcase and had a Red Cross on the lid. "I heard you might of cut yourself."

"Who said I might have cut myself?"

"Rennie Cross."

"That prick."

"Jimmy Shattuck said you tried to cut him with a beer bottle, Walter. He showed me the bandage on his belly over at the emergency room, but said he wasn't going to press charges."

"Go to hell with your first-aid kit," I said. "You're just playing cop."

"Now, Walter, you know I don't like that word."

The dog whined and leaned forward. I thought he was going to come for me then. Billy mumbled something and he sat back on his haunches. He still was ready, though.

"Caesar don't like rough language," Billy said calmly. "He associates it with lowlifes."

"Nobody likes what I've got to say tonight."

I was beginning to feel silly, braced on my hands in the bed mouthing off at this big cop and his giant dog. My head was hurting and my eyes wouldn't stop watering. My side was stinging a lot worse, too. I could taste blood in my mouth.

"Ah, to hell with it," I said, and laid back down.

The room went all dark and fuzzy, and the next thing I knew I felt cold air on my midsection and my belt being undone. I opened my eyes and Billy was hitched up beside the bed in a kitchen chair, tugging my shirttail out of my pants.

"You passed out."

"Go to hell."

"Sure, sure," he said peacefully. He got the shirt and sweater back out of the way. I could see dried blood on the bunched clothing. I couldn't see past them. "You'll live," he said.

"Big deal."

"Yeah. Just a couple sliced places and a kind of gouged out spot with a lump of skin still in it."

"Jesus. You going to write a book report on it?"

"Tough, huh?" he said. "Here, this'll do you some

good, then." He tilted a brown bottle over me, and it was like he'd punched me and set me on fire at once. I let out a yell and jumped to get away. That damn dog came charging in from the sun porch showing a mouthful of teeth. Billy sent him back. He didn't want to go.

"Lucky you had your sweater on," Billy said. "It picked up most of the splinters. You better get it off before they work through and cut you, though. You probably ought to think about a tetanus shot, too, this being Florida and all. I'll bandage it up for you, for now." He started in.

"Why the special treatment?"

"They say you went crazy and threatened to shoot 'em," he said. "That don't sound like you, Walter. I thought I better check on you. You get that big mouse on your cheek and that swollen ear and them cuts on your mouth from falling down somewhere?"

"Ask Shattuck."

"That's what I thought. You scared that ol' boy pretty good, Walter. Did you threaten to shoot him?"

"There were two of them. Lennie Cross, too. I thought they were going to follow me outside and stomp me. I had to say something."

Billy grinned. "That's about what I thought. Pretty quick thinking, there, Walter. That's what they thought, too, after they had time to think about it. Now everybody will be laughing at them because you scared them with a bluff. Did they start it?"

"What do you think?"

"Yeah, well, Jimmy Shattuck's always been a blowhard and a bully. He's started things before, all right. They never turned out like this for him, though. He may have to look you up for scaring him in front of people. You call his busted flush or something?"

"It wasn't about cards."

"Uh-huh. That's just about what I was afraid of," he

115

said.

"What do you mean?"

"Old man Valland called the cab company and said they'd better be sure one of their taxis brought his daughter home from Dawson's every single night from now on. Said he'd come down there and clean them out if they didn't. Everybody on the Beaches knows who Bull is cutting out of the action, Walter. You two weren't all that discreet, driving all over the Beaches at night."

"Everybody ought to mind their own business," I said.

"Valland's making it everybody's business. Walk careful, Walter. Valland is real bad news like Shattuck never even dreamed of being." Billy had water in a glass and some aspirin. "Here, take these and drink all the water. You look dehydrated. Shock, probably."

I did what he said. The water seemed to absorb into my mouth and throat and spread a coolness in my belly.

"How can Valland get away with shit like threatening the taxi company?"

"Well, he's just too mean a man to cross for no good reason. Also, he's got a lot of the right friends."

"Who, for instance?"

"Well, me for instance." He closed his case and stood up. "That should hold you. You may want to see a doctor. You ought to get that sweater off."

"Okay," I said. I was half going to sleep again. My side had gone numb from the stuff he put on it. "Thanks for the bandages. You're all right, Billy."

"Yeah. You're okay yourself, Walter. I always thought so. You always did mind your own business. But you got to take it easy now until this blows over. I'll shut off the lights and lock up behind me. You shouldn't forget to lock your door behind you if you're going to play with tough boys like Shattuck and Cross."

Chapter Nineteen

I don't know how long after Billy Jarvis left that I finally woke up. It was raining steadily so I couldn't guess by the sun, and my wristwatch had run down at quarter past three. My alarm clock had stopped at seven thirty. The cloud cover made it dark outside, but it didn't look like morning, so the alarm clock had probably wound down while I slept the whole morning away. With the steady slow tap of rain on the roof and both the clock and the watch wound down, it was almost like life had paused to give me a breather.

North Florida winter rain is not like the wild thunderstorms that tourists see in the summer. Unless there's a Northeaster blowing, or a hurricane passing by offshore to stir things up, winter rain on the North Coast just starts falling out of a dirty grey sky and keeps on falling for a long time, steady and slow, like there's a leak somewhere in heaven. By November the waterlogged trunks of the palm trees turn almost black. They used to say you could tell it's winter on the Beaches when the trunks of the palm trees turned from dry brown to soggy black.

I stayed in bed and dozed some more without any bad dreams. I felt warm and safe because I didn't have to go in to work today. The rain on the roof was good music to sleep by, with all the night terrors gone.

Sometimes that November rain seemed cold enough to turn into sleet but it almost never did. Old timers told me it had snowed on the Beaches only once in living memory. It stayed on the ground until noontime. All the schools let out for the kids to play in it. I hoped that if this rain turned to snow over near Lake City her grandparents would let Sally stay home to play in it. There was a better chance for snow inland because temperatures got colder away from the ocean. Sally was a South Florida baby and never had seen snow.

The winter rain made the Beaches seem peaceful and quiet. I missed rain like that when I lived in Tampa and St. Pete, where it was either big afternoon thunderstorms or more sunshine than you could stand. This North Florida rain was like winter rain I grew up with in Ohio. But for the palm trees outside my apartment it could have been Ohio or Pennsylvania rain, or Pacific Northwest rain or German rain over in Frankfurt where I slung hash in a repo depot after the war.

It rained a lot, and snowed too, the two winters I was a mess sergeant in Germany for a transient population of GIs rotating in and out of Europe. Frankfurt still was pretty beat up from the fighting when I was there. My sleeping billet was in an old stone building that still had bullet pocks around the windows where the Wehrmacht made their last stand.

Today, thinking about Germany kind of surprised me. I didn't usually think about Germany much, or the Army. Somehow the rain brought it all back. My eyes and my feet kept me out of the war and I wasn't called up until the shooting was over. Then they just ran me through Basic Training and put me right back in a kitchen. The Army was okay, really. Sometimes, like now, I wondered vaguely why I didn't stay in. They didn't bother cooks much, and a kitchen is a kitchen. When you were off duty you could do just about anything you wanted to do. I liked sitting in *gasthauses* drinking real German beer and listening to the Germans talk. Never a Nazi among any of them, of course. All the Nazis were dead or in South America it seemed. I figured everyday Germans had to say whatever it took to get by, like most people, and didn't hold it against them. I really liked some of those German fräuleins. They were short of eligible German males, too, courtesy of the Allies. I might even have wound up marrying a fräuleins if I stayed in the army. But I met Chris when I got back to the States and I didn't stay in, so that was that. Which kind of circled me back to thinking of Sally and the possibility of snow in Lake City.

It's funny how when there's a big shakeup in your life, and you know things aren't going to be the same anymore, you find yourself dredging up all the old memories you can think of. Good ones and sad ones, important ones and silly ones, almost like you're trying to remember exactly who you were before the big change. It's almost like your memories might be strong enough to make your life stay the same, not changed forever by what just happened.

It was very pleasant there under the covers with the rain tapping, half dozing and half-remembering and feeling safe. I hated to let the feeling go, but I already had slept a long time. I wasn't even sure how long. My mouth felt almost gummed shut. I had sweated while I slept and my crotch and armpits were clammy and damp. The pillow under the back of my neck was damp, too. I was stinking so bad I could smell myself. All the kitchen odors in my clothes, and the stale spilled beer on top of kitchen grease, had turned rancid. My mouth tasted like a bean fart smells. My socks were stuck to my feet and felt like they had sand in them.

I was hungry too. I hate to be both hungry and dirty at the same time. I wanted to stay in bed and listen to the rain on the roof and hold onto that feeling of being safe, but being hungry and dirty at the same time wouldn't let me. I didn't want to get out from under the covers but I wanted a hot shower real bad. I wondered if the bandage Billy had fixed would come off in the shower.

Thinking about those cuts that Billy had doctored made me restless. I started to pick at the edges of the adhesive tape under the covers. One end came loose. I couldn't make it stick back down. The stuff Billy had poured on the cuts was the only clean smell in the room. Out on the screen porch, my old Duotherm heater gurgled and the blower kicked in for a minute. The temperature must be dropping off colder. I couldn't even remember firing the heater up last night. I was pretty sure I was almost out of last year's fuel oil.

Once I finally got up and got moving it didn't seem so cold in the apartment. I stuffed my dirty clothes in the hamper and got in the shower quick. I stood with my mouth wide open and let the shower blast some of the bad taste. The water was as hot as I could stand it. The bandage got soaked and started rubbing against the edges of my cuts so I wadded it up and threw it on the floor. The Mercurochrome made the whole area of skin where the bandage had been bright orange and it didn't wash off. The cuts were dry and sucked-up looking. I kept the spray from hitting it the best I could and stayed in there until the hot water ran out. Then I brushed my teeth and shaved and put on clean pants and a fresh T-shirt, and a clean sweater. I let the Venetian blinds up and cranked the porch jalousies partway open. The cold air seemed to hesitate outside the wet screens before coming in. The air smelled of rain and the sea. I turned off the heater to save the rest of the oil, and stripped the bed. There were bloodstains on the sheets. I put the sheets in the hamper and spread the bedcovers over the porch furniture to air out.

I fried Spam and eggs in black butter and perked a pot of coffee to take the edge off my hunger and began to feel halfway human. By now Billy and his Great Dane, and all the rest of it, seemed like some bad dream. I got the soggy bandage and put it in the garbage. I figured the clean T-shirt was as good as a fresh bandage for protecting the cuts. Let them breathe some. I didn't need any doctor and couldn't afford one anyway.

I called the telephone recording that sang you a song about buying a boat through the First National Bank and then told you the correct time, and wound up my wristwatch and my alarm clock. It was 4:36 p.m. I called Ramsey's Fuel Oil and got their answering service. I asked the lady at the service to take a request for ten dollars worth of fuel oil and said I would leave the money in my mailbox for the oil truck guy. Puttering around like that helped keep my mind off what had happened last night.

When I got ready to leave the apartment, I got out my old wool herringbone sport coat that I bought in Philadelphia with some of my Army separation pay. You don't get much chance to wear Harris Tweed in Florida and it was another way to hold off thinking about what happened last night.

I drove the Chev around town slow to let it warm up good. I wasn't looking for anybody and in fact kind of hoped I didn't see anybody I knew. What I think I was doing was trying to prove to myself that nothing had really changed and there was no reason not to just go on with my life like normal.

Rainy days kind of sewed places and times together in my mind so I could really see that the whole world was part of a piece. Even out in the Chev driving around it still felt peaceful and calm, and memories kept surprising me. There was a section of Cincinnati down toward the Ohio River where I started cooking all those years ago that in the rain resembled parts of Jacksonville along the St. Johns. There was a bar in Cincinnati called Sy's where I used to hang out that was almost exactly like a tavern in a jerkwater little town called Olympia out in the Pacific Northwest where I played shuffleboard and drank an obscure local beer named after the town.

I closed out my Army stint at Camp Lewis after I rotated back from Germany. Nights and weekends I slung hash for a retired master sergeant at an off-post joint he owned. I had married Chris on furlough back home to Ohio and she moved to the Northwest with me. It rained steady, summer and winter, the whole time we were there. Chris hated it and said it made her cough all the time and feel feverish. This was before the TB. After the time we spent out there Chris wanted sunshine forever, so we wound up in Tampa and then Saint Pete. No matter what the doctors told her later, Chris always blamed her TB on Washington State.

I drove south toward St. Augustine on Highway A1A, the pavement slick and shiny in the rain and almost deserted. There was no ocean wind at all. I used to think that nothing really bad could happen to you in that kind of calm, straight-down rain. Cops who ducked the rain in various joints where I cooked over the years told me that even cat burglars took the night off in this kind of rain, and the knifings and family beatings dropped off. Cars seemed to run smoother in that kind of rain too, something about combustion and the Chev just purred going toward St. Augustine.

I was just trying to think about everything else in the world except what had happened with Rennie Cross and Shattuck last night, and what might happen today, but would certainly happen sooner or later. Billy was right that Shattuck would be after me. Shattuck would figure I had made him back down in front of witnesses and his reputation as a bully would be on the line.

When I finally let myself think about it, I saw that I had made Shattuck back down. Rennie, too. They deserved it, for what they said about Corinne. For a minute I felt pretty good about making them back down. But I was pretty sure that Shattuck couldn't just let it be. He would have to fix me for sticking that bottle in him and making him back down. He'd have to fix me so everybody knew about it.

Whatever Shattuck did next wouldn't even be about Corinne anymore, it would be about me sticking him and making him back down. He wouldn't just be out for some mean fun with Rennie like he had been last night. He would be dead serious next time. He didn't just need to show everybody on the Beaches what a mistake I made to cross him, he needed to prove it to himself too. Because I scared him badly with that broken bottle, and no bully could let something like that go by from a runt like me. He had to re establish himself.

My face still felt lopsided where Shattuck had punched me the first time and my ear was swollen where his second punch had landed. When I touched my ear, just like that, I had a flashback to how easily Shattuck had knocked me down. My face began to throb with the thought of him ever getting hold of me again. Shattuck would have to hurt me really badly to be able to forget that I made him back down. He might even stomp me after he got me down.

The peaceful feeling the rain had given me of time suspended was long gone by now. I realized how tight my neck was when I turned my head to glance out the rear-view mirror. I was so spooked I was expecting to see Shattuck's No. 8 cab coming after me.

I thought about the cab because that's really the only thing I knew about Shattuck was that he drove a taxi. I didn't even know if he had a car of his own, or what it looked like if he did. I didn't really know anything about him but his reputation for meanness, and hadn't ever wanted to know anything about him.

I was south of the Oasis by then, all alone on A1A, and it was still raining. I tell myself now that I didn't know where I intended to go when I started driving south that day. That I really wasn't intending to go anywhere until I reached the Palm Valley Road. But I turned off west just the same, like I had been headed that way all along.

I was good and spooked again by then. Okay, I was spooked. I wasn't ashamed of being afraid of somebody as tough as Shattuck. So I would go where I had some tough friends of my own, where Shattuck would never think of showing his face, friends who were tougher than Shattuck ever dreamed of being. Whether he had his own car or not, Shattuck would never try to follow me where I was going. And the last thing I needed was to have to deal with Shattuck or Rennie Cross again so soon after last night.

Chapter Twenty

*H*eaded away from the ocean on the Palm Valley Road, you are in a different Florida from the tourist brochures. There are big hardwoods and a lot of live oaks that reach across the pavement. The shade is deep in summer and the branches are bare and awkward-looking through the short winter. I was always told that the cypress out there was Spanish plantings gone wild.

The Spanish were going to tame Florida like they did California and Mexico and South America. They even put in rice paddies along here over on the backwaters of the Tolomato River where there was just gators and duck grass and bigmouth bass when I got here. They ran cattle here before there was ever a single longhorn in Texas. There was a Spanish Trail that ran through Palm Valley from St. Augustine to the St. Johns River. The Spaniards did their usual number on the local Indians, and once slaughtered a bunch of Frenchmen under Jean Ribault who tried to encroach on their territory. They planted exotic trees to shade the haciendas they were going to build. They came to stay. But Florida and first the English and then American colonists ran them out. The English and the colonists took all the credit for chasing them back to Madrid, but my money would be on Florida.

In the 1950s, rutted little roads led back off the Palm Valley Road to tin-roofed shacks. The people out there scratched a living out of truck gardens and a cash crop of moonshine. They stuck to themselves and the government mostly left them alone. They would have been hillbillies if there had been a real hill within three hundred miles. Their granddaddies used to drive buckboards out to the coast and surf-fish until the tide dropped so they could get into St. Augustine for supplies on the hard sand. They couldn't keep a wagon road cut through the undergrowth then, or didn't try. Didn't try was more likely.

When the Corps of Engineers dredged the Tolomato River into part of the Inland Waterway, they could get into St. Augustine by boat then and of course there was A1A then too. When bird feathers and alligator leather were in high fashion, and Prohibition was on, they lived high and paid cash for hot Mercury V-8s and unplugged Browning automatic shotguns. To this day they still poached gators for vacation money or to finance a new still. They seldom sent a boy of theirs to a "guvment war," because they considered it damn foolishness to shoot at strangers unless they were trespassing.

West of Palm Valley, you came suddenly upon the humpback little Corps of Engineers drawbridge across the Waterway. There were docks and fuel below the bridge for the rich Yankee yachts that traveled the Waterway all the way from New England. I did a few weekend shifts of backup cooking at The Anchorage restaurant down there behind the docks before I caught on full-time with Dawson's. The clientele on weekends was yacht crews in expensive casual wear and Palm Valley families in their Sunday clothes from the Sears, Roebuck and Montgomery Ward catalogs.

When I crossed the bridge, there was a big blue-and-white sedan cruiser at the fuel docks and guys in yellow oilskins fuelling her. It reminded me of a daydream I used to have that some passing yachtsman would like my cooking and hire me aboard for the season.

Past the Waterway, wide grazing pastures dotted with scrub pine took over and the land began to resemble like East Texas. Metal posters nailed to gates by the Florida Cattlemen's Association gleamed in the rain where my headlights hit them, offering rewards for cattle rustlers just like out west. The big Florida beef combines quarantined their out-of-state breeding stock here before moving it to their bigger spreads. A couple of range detectives I used to feed weekend breakfast at the Anchorage said the Palm Valley crowd considered the combines' prime beef like a grocery store when they couldn't poach a deer. The detectives were partly right, but hadn't figured out yet that most of the rustled beef went in the back doors of big restaurants for cents on the dollar below market price.

After a few miles of range fence, I saw the state fire tower up ahead that guarded the timber company flatwoods that edged the cattle range. Then there was the flicker of headlights going north and south on the big dual highway. It was almost full dusk. After I got out into the traffic, it was only two miles south to the Below The Border truck stop. There were eight or ten out-of-state cars in front, winter tourists headed for Miami, and maybe thirty big rigs lined up in the muddy truck lot. That rumor about truck stops having the best food was never going to die. The Below The Border qualified, though, with Donlevy running the kitchen.

I noticed a couple of Florida cars against some of the tourist cabins on the far side of the restaurant, backed in to conceal their license plates from cruising private detectives. Florida only ran one license plate back then. I recognized one of the cars as being from the Beaches. It looked like everybody was doing it but me. *Doin' it, doin' it,* like in the song. I went on into the restaurant.

The cashier was a big oily man no taller than me but shaped like a pear. He had slick black wavy hair, and skin grease almost leaked out of his big pores. It made his face gleam in the yellow light.

"Walder!" he yelled. "Hiya, fella!"

"I'm okay, Ronnie. Donlevy on tonight?"

"He'ds always on, Walder, he'ds always on, one way or anudder." Ronnie always talked with a nasty nasal drip.

"He working, then?"

"Course, he's worgink. Duh *touristas,* dey're on duh road to duh big M buh you know dat. Godda geeb 'em fed!"

"The tourists seem to be missing the Beaches."

"Dey been missing duh Beeges for years, Walder. Whad's new? Wade dil duh spressways get done! Den duh Beeges dry ub an' blow uhway.

"I know, I know."

"Dat crazy Dawson! He really tryin' to stay oben all winder?"

"Yeah."

"Wen he goes broge, cumb see me." He laughed, showing a lot of gold in his teeth. With his skin color, he looked like a comic-opera bandit. It wasn't too bad a description. He leaned over and lowered his voice. "You deed somb cash? Wan'da run somb *bolita* for me?"

I couldn't help it. I shot a quick glance around.

He laughed out loud. "You god a guildy conscious, Walder, you bad boy you!"

"Just stop with that. I can't afford anything like that now. I ain't cut out for it. I got no nerve."

"C'mon, Walder. You can'd blay duh dogs on whad Dawson bays you."

"How well I know. I'm not playing the greyhounds these days."

"I dond't blame you, Walder! You stard boking holes in windbags you gonna need all duh lug you can find, widout playing duh dogs."

"Word sure gets around," I said. "Tell Donlevy I want his shrimps, and no damn tourist order, either. I'm half starving to death. And tell Jeannie to make me a pitcher of fresh ice tea. She's the only one can make it half like

Mama."

"Mama?"

"Mrs. Bull Valland," I said.

"Ho boy, Walder, the dotter and the mamba doo?

"Jesus, Ronnie – get yourself some nasal spray. And stop smirking like a damn greaseball."

He was laughing so hard his eyes were wet. He honked his nose on a big silk handkerchief. "Man, you musta growed a dew sed of balls, Walder. I *am* a greaseball, bud id's not nice to say."

"Just tell Donlevy I want to see him when he gets a minute, okay?"

"Hokay, tiger," he said.

Donlevy came out to my booth after I finished eating. He was a big wide character with thick black hair on his forearms and crawling up out of the neck of his shirt. He moved like a bulldozer, but somehow his white shirts never lost their starch in the kitchen, and he always looked like he just came on shift. He was a formally trained chef, some West Coast school, and he was quite a lady-killer.

He slid in across from me and started stuffing a big bulldog pipe I had never seen him without. "It is zo rare we 'ave ze plaisir to serve ze gourmet of so rare sensitivity," he said.

"C'mon, that sounds awful in your bullfrog voice."

He looked wounded. "The gals all think my voice is sexy."

"Save it for them, then."

"You laid any good stuff lately?"

I felt the tightness start up right away. That was silly here. That was always the first question Donlevy asked anyone, male or female. Some of the females even found it cute. Getting laid and mixing marijuana with his custom pipe tobacco were about the only things in life that held Donlevy's interest besides food preparation. But the tightness came up anyway.

"Drop that line of crap," I said.

He leaned back and puffed his pipe. I couldn't smell anything funny, just the strong Latakia, so maybe it was straight tobacco this time, but it wouldn't be the first time he'd smoked Mary Jane right out in the open restaurant. He was grinning around his pipe stem.

"Well, I'll be damned," he said. "So you got a sweetheart at last. About damn time, too."

"Now cut it out," I said. "I mean it. I didn't have to come all the way out here to put up with that crap. I can get that on the Beaches. Plenty of it. Too much of it."

"Okay." He kept grinning. "Why did you come out here? Just to eat my superior cooking?"

"To buy a gun."

He stopped grinning and puffed some more on his pipe. "Serious, huh?" he said finally.

"Dead serious."

"You show a certain turn of phrase, my boy." He tamped his pipe. "I thought you had a gun. You even told certain people you had one. You shouldn't tell that kind of people you're heeled when you're not."

"Is that all anybody's been talking about since last night?"

"Just a little excitement to spice up our dull lives," Donlevy said. "You always said restaurant people tend to live vicariously, having no lives of their own."

"If you know all about it you know I'm in a fix here," I said.

"You scared 'em good, Walter. You did for a fact. There's a few--a few gamblers here and there--who remember that you used to do a few errands for Ronnie around the Beaches before you went to Dawson's. That's why everybody in that motel room believed you about the hardware. Shattuck and Cross will probably lay off you now."

"Not if they find out I was lying, they won't."

"You shouldn't tell lies, Walter. I've told you that before. I bet your mother told you, too." It was just Donlevy being Donlevy. He amused himself, mostly. "Didn't you ever have a Sunday school teacher up there in Ohio? It's always worse for liars in the end."

I waited until I was sure he was through having his fun. "If I get a gun, I won't be a liar," I said. "How much? Remember, I'm not rich. I've got expenses." Donlevy knew all about the TB and the raw deal I got in Saint Pete.

Donlevy was relighting his pipe, almost hidden behind clouds of blue smoke. When he had it going good he looked up again. "Somebody tells me Shattuck sicced Billy on you last night, Walter. How come you're out walking around?"

"Somebody knows an awful lot around here."

"Didn't your mother ever tell you the night has a thousand eyes, Walter?" He puffed on his pipe and smiled quietly. "You were raised poorly, I tell you."

"So why do you ask about Billy?" I said.

"Well, Walter, did Billy, like, warn you not to try to buy a gun?"

"No."

"Did Billy, like, tell you he wouldn't bust you for sticking that bottle in Shattuck if you would roll over for him and hand him something worth an arrest like an under-the-table gun dealer?"

"You know I wouldn't do something like that!" I was getting mad. "That's bullshit."

"Then why come out here? Why not just go buy one over the counter, no one the wiser?" This was before all the laws and computers so it would have been that simple in those days. But I had my reasons.

"I can't trust some hardware store clerk not to

mention me buying a gun. I don't want anybody to ever know that I didn't have one with me last night. It's bad enough that I didn't let them beat the shit out of me. It'll be a lot worse if they find out I made that kind of fools out of both of them."

Donlevy sighed. "I wish I had gone over to play poker last night. I would like to have been there to see it. Of course I wouldn't have let them walk on you too bad."

"I wish you'd been there, too, because I wouldn't be here now if you had been. They probably wouldn't have even tried it with you there."

He nodded at that. "You're sure Billy didn't send you out here?"

"You know me better than that, Donlevy."

"I did, once. That was B.C. Before Corinne. That's her name, right? I can't help worry about Billy, Walter. He's got a hero complex. It's been six, seven years since him and that first Great Dane of his stopped three bank robbers headed for Mayport with sixty thou. They were gonna take a shrimper out to meet a tramp ship they had a deal with."

"Pretty smart."

"Not smart enough, because they had to drive through Billy's turf. He remembers strange faces around the Beaches. When Jacksonville broadcast the description of the robbers, those little light bulbs went on in his head. He was waiting on the Mayport road when they came through. He killed two and the Dane got the other one. They got the Dane and put a couple buckshot in Billy. Hero stuff. He loved it. Maybe he'd like to hand the District Attorney a nice little operation like mine until something fancier comes along."

"Go fuck yourself." I started to get up.

"What do you want?"

"Huh?"

"I mean a .38, a .45, what?"

"I thought you weren't going to do business with me."

"Just showing you what's going on in the world around you, Walter. You mind your own business too much. You truly are the last of the innocents. That's why nobody ever tumbled to you as a numbers runner."

"Get screwed."

"A more reasonable thought than your first suggestion," he agreed. "I guarantee you that I will take getting screwed under advisement. You want to wear it or leave it in the car most of the time?"

"The car. What'll it cost?"

"For you, fifty bucks."

It was a lot, but it had to be done. "What do I get?"

"A very ordinary old gun, complete with some spot rust and chips in the handle. As if you'd had it for *ages*."

"Will it shoot?"

He just shook his head at me. "You're tense, so I'm going to ignore that remark in the name of friendship, Walter. It'll shoot. Since your enemies seem to come king-size, I'm going to suggest a .45."

"You mean like Mike Hammer?"

"The caliber, yes. The gun, no. A revolver's simpler. An auto is a pro's gun. Too many things to remember. The revolver you just point and pull. An old Colt's double action revolver with what the British call a sawn barrel. War surplus. I'll throw in one box of 50 rounds and four half-moon clips."

"What the hell is a half-moon clip?"

"An adapter so you can use the .45 automatic shells in a revolver."

"That doesn't sound simple to me."

"Believe me, it's very simple. Easy to master."

"Okay. When can I have it?"

"Tomorrow. Bring small used bills of course. And

Walter? All friendship and kidding aside, if Billy gets onto me through you it's not going to be your lucky day."

"Some friendship, to pull a threat like that," I said.

"Business is business, Walter."

Chapter Twenty-One

Sunday midday it was still raining when I drove out to the Below the Border before my shift at Dawson's. I had gone straight home and to bed the night before, expecting to see Shattuck's cab down every side street. Rain on the roof lulled me to sleep and if I hadn't ached all over my face and where the broken bottle had cut me, I almost could have believed none of it had happened at all.

Donlevy and I had coffee in his kitchen and talked about nothing in particular until it was time for me to go and he walked me out, carrying a small brown paper sack. He sat with me in the Chev over by the motel units, empty this time of day, and took a roll of oily cloth out of the sack. He checked me out on the gun right there in the car. He showed me that the Colt's cylinder rotated clockwise, saying he didn't want me to be surprised in case I was familiar with a Smith & Wesson's counter-clockwise spin. I never had thought about which way revolver cylinders rotate. I told him the only pistol I'd ever qualified on was a 1911Government Model auto, something the Army made cooks do for some reason or other, and he said hell he wished I'd told him that and he could have got me an automatic for 75 dollars. I told him the revolver would do. The only thing I knew about revolvers was from watching old gangster movies on television but I didn't say that since Donlevy was kind of a small-time gangster himself.

The rain was making washtub drum rolls on the car roof and the windows were fogged. Nobody could have figured out what we were doing without being in the Chev with us. Donlevy was a hell of a cook, and a very careful crook. I'd seen him take all the precautions even when he pulled off the smallest fence out the back door of the restaurant. The people he did business with respected him and shuffled reliable people to him, and he did likewise. He helped out the little people who were looking for things they couldn't find in the Yellow Pages. His specialty was guns. It was just a thing you knew, and never needed to know. But sometimes it turned out you did.

He fitted the fat .45 automatic shells into those funny little half-moon adapters for the revolver, holding each cartridge carefully with the oily rag.

"Sometimes a man needs a friend to get him through the night," he said. He folded the big cylinder into the gun and handed it to me butt-first. "Shake hands with your new friend, Walter."

"Don't make it a big thing," I said.

"Okay," he said. "Just wait and see. You don't have to wait until you get hemmed in and really need your new friend. Just see if you don't feel a little more three-dimensional out there on that miserable road to the Beaches on this miserable wet day. Now I will set here while you wipe everything down again with this oily rag, and then give them back to me. The paper sack is yours. Some cops are silly enough to dust guns and cartridges for fingerprints if they happen across them."

I paid him and told him he was being paranoid, but I wiped the Colt and the ammunition and the ammunition box down anyway. I put the gun back in the paper sack and under my front seat, perfectly legal in Florida in those days, and put the box of remaining shells and the two extra adapters in the glove box.

All the way back to the Beaches I kept thinking about what Donlevy had said, and he was right. I kept telling myself that it was silly to feel braver now. I hadn't even tested the damn thing yet to see if it actually fired. Not that Donlevy would palm off a dud on me. But it was a cozy feeling driving back toward the Beaches with that big old Parkerized Colt under the seat. The best way I can describe it is that it was kind of like knowing you had a good serviceable spare tire in the trunk, and the right tire jack. You might not ever need it, but if you did, nothing else would do.

The rain kept up steadily all Sunday night. We had a lot of the people come in to Dawson's who were the kind that only the rain brings out. There were couples who probably believed dinner at the Beaches in the rain was romantic because of some movie they'd seen. There were other couples from the city who really couldn't afford to be seen together in public at all. They tended to get washed in, too, with the rain. Without even knowing the details, you could just tell. For some reason we sold a lot of shrimp dinners that night. Funny the things that stick in memory.

When those backstreet couples started showing up in Dawson's that November, he began to really think that staying open after August was going to work. In summer, those kinds of couples usually showed up on weekdays after a thunderstorm, when it was a pretty good bet the only patrons would be families on vacation from Alabama or Georgia or somewhere else. They rented those old fashioned little separated beach cottages with a garage unit for the car, and backed it in to hide the plate. You could just about bet the name in the tourist court office didn't match the car's registration.

We were close enough to Navy bases to get a Marine or sailor or two, alone, in PX civvies and one of those plastic military raincoats, trying to pretend for the night they were free civilians. I had done the same thing in Germany. The young military guys usually ordered a Captain's Platter and lots of beer, making a night of it.

There were also the singles with closed faces, used to being alone all the time, who suddenly could not stand whatever solitude they could usually stand very well until the rains came on.

The restaurant was pretty busy all night. I had my special snapper chowder on simmer, and even threw together a rain hash I learned to make in Cincinnati that you wouldn't expect to find in a seafood joint. The customers were real rain people. A lot of them ordered chowder or the hash. The kitchen was warm and full of nostalgic smells and I was the boss, and what I did could make or break their rainy night for the customers. It was a heavy, comfortable responsibility, knowing the food they ordered on a night like this wasn't just about belly hunger.

The way they ordered, the combinations, had rain in it. They needed to travel out through the rain someplace warm with bright lights and eat a solid meal, and then go home through the rain again, warm and full and satisfied. Some of them were locals who walked over from their apartment on the boardwalk for fish and chips and coffee, and were going right back to their book or television. I had two requests that night for Eggs Maxim, and they were tickled pink when I knew how to do them.

It was a great night by winter standards and Dawson was beside himself with pleasure. He brought back several compliments from the floor. He ate my rain hash for dinner himself and asked if I would make him a couple quarts for his deer camp after Thanksgiving. He was relaxed and happy about word getting around that we didn't close after Labor Day. One couple had drive all the way down from Folkston, Georgia, just for a special Sunday dinner. Pray for sunshiny weather, Dawson said, and we'll really be in business. I didn't argue with him, but there were some things even Dawson still didn't understand about why people go out to restaurants.

Corinne had Sundays off, so I had the chance to move in the kitchen without being distracted by all that. I was able for the most part to forget about my fight with Rennie and Shattuck. My simple midnight-diner twists on seafood standards got the most compliments, pretty exciting in a famous seafood restaurant. Greasy spoon stuff, done my way. I had watched a lot of night rain outside a lot of diner windows learning to cook stuff people wouldn't ever forget.

I hoped the rain would last until I got home and to bed, and it did. I went to sleep listening to it tapping on the roof, with the Colt under my pillow. It was my best night's sleep in a long time. When Mabel woke me up Monday, it was still raining. Dawson must not have been giving his tithe to the church that year.

Chapter Twenty-Two

*I*t rained the whole week leading up to Thanksgiving. The weather bureau said the rain was the only thing holding off the first real cold snap of winter. The temperature stayed in the forties and fifties. The sports writers in Jacksonville were writing about how wet the Gator Bowl field was and comparing Georgia's and Florida's records on muddy fields. People coming in the restaurant tracked water and mud everywhere and the busboys had to mop all night.

Customers used every old joke about weather fit for ducks that I ever heard. Dawson said they were crazy because ducks only moved on a storm front with wind and dropping barometer. Dawson was a dyed-in-the-wool hunter, ducks and deer and quail and anything else you could name, and couldn't wait for hunting season to start after Thanksgiving.

Other than making his hunting plans, he was in a sour mood because he knew the slow steady rain wasn't really any good for ducks and he just flat didn't believe it was good for the restaurant business. All the duck jokes, and the fact the rain just kept on falling, had him irritable in spite of the fact that the customers kept coming in. The other thing that had him all wound up was the thing that year about cranberries.

He was advertising a home-style turkey buffet with all the trimmings, eat all you want But there was some kind of government scare that traces of a cancer-causing weed-killer had been found in the cranberry crop, and it looked like nobody was going to get cranberry sauce that year. It was the first time there had ever been a scare like that, and

I couldn't find a single supplier with cranberries, or willing to admit they had any, so I couldn't make my real cranberry sauce.

As far as Dawson was concerned it wasn't Thanksgiving without cranberries. I tried to sell him on a blueberry cobbler, since cranberries and blueberries are the only native North American fruits besides Concord grapes. Theoretically the Pilgrims could have had blueberries, and we could say that on the menu. He finally okayed the blueberry idea at almost the last minute, which made me have to scramble, but he never stopped acting like it was all part of a conspiracy to bankrupt him for trying to stay open straight through. He would have been open for Thanksgiving anyway, so the cranberries still would have been a problem, but you couldn't tell that to Dawson.

I had more logistics to worry about that blueberry cobbler. We had a stack of frozen birds in the walk-in, and I stayed until midnight the night before in on prep work and then was in the kitchen by 4:30 a.m. to get things going. I had both the other cooks in early, and Dawson was there before seven.

He was in some state, all right, what they called in Florida a shit-and-a-sweat. . He had laid on heavy newspaper and radio advertising in Jacksonville, going after the Georgia football money like he did every year, even when he stayed closed after Labor Day until the Thanksgiving Day game. He had corsages made up of phony flowers in Georgia and Florida team colors for the waitresses to wear, and special place mats with Bulldogs and Gators on them. He already had special Thanksgiving souvenir menus printed, and had to make the busboys staple on a one-page mimeo sheet to explain the cranberry problem and blueberry substitution. Long before the game even started, he had a big red banner hung over the front entrance saying Florida Welcomes The Bulldogs. It got waterlogged and came down before kickoff.

I asked Corinne if she was rooting for the Bulldogs since she was from Georgia, and she said football was a waste of time. She said what those football coaches did to those poor boys for training was almost as bad as what the Marines did to recruits on Paris Island. But when the busboys started a pool on the game, she got in for a dollar. She took Georgia and six. She lost.

It was a bad year for the Georgia Bulldogs. They had injuries. Even when they got some of their players healthy, they hadn't been much write home about that year. The Gators that year weren't all that terrific either, which made Thanksgiving a lot worse for the Georgia faithful because the Gators just plain stomped the hell out of the Bulldogs in the rain. The final score was one of those things that look like a misprint in the newspaper. The diehard fans who had stuck with the Bulldogs through a bad year, and come all that way to sit in the cold wet Gator Bowl, thought they at least deserved a win over Florida to repay them for their loyalty.

They must have been shell-shocked. One Jacksonville sportswriter said Georgia fans got out of town like Napoleon leaving Moscow. They must never have wanted to see an orange juice commercial again as long as they lived. The wet weather just made them miserable and the loss broke their spirit, and they didn't feel like going to the Beaches to party. They just went home. So there we sat with the restaurant full of turkey smell and all those trimmings coming out of the oven about the time the first tour buses should have been arriving, and the only thing in the big side parking lot was puddles. In past years the Georgia fans who had come all the way to Jacksonville for the game would want to make a weekend out of it at the Beaches, win or lose, but almost nobody showed up.

We did get a surge of Florida fans from the Gainesville area and they were happy and felt like spending money, but they never filled the place up. We got a surprising number of locals who didn't want to cook their own turkeys, and some Navy families from out at the Mayport base, but we had an awful lot of turkey left. Before we closed, Dawson told us to divide up what was left between us. I took home enough white meat for a couple weeks of sandwiches, and a lot of dressing, and a pan of cobbler. Nobody makes better turkey dressing than me. This is a simple statement of fact. I liked to eat it cold from the refrigerator, or warmed up with my giblet gravy. It looked like I was going to eat pretty good at home for a couple of weeks. I always had liked holiday leftovers better than the main event.

Dawson probably broke pretty close to even when all was said and done. But it probably was going to take him a while to get over feeling like Florida was conspiring to ruin him, just because he broke tradition and stayed open after August. The day after Thanksgiving he said it was time to cut his losses and posted a new schedule to stay open only Tuesdays and Wednesdays and weekends through Christmas.

Corinne still took the taxi home every night. I hadn't heard a peep out of Shattuck or Rennie Cross. I noticed that Cab No. 8 picked her up a couple of times. That was Shattuck's cab and it made me so mad that I was almost sick to think of her riding in the same car with him, after what he'd said about her. But there was nothing I could do about it.

Corinne and I didn't say a lot to each other anymore. She didn't ask me about the fight with Shattuck, or about the beer bottle, so I guess she didn't know about it then. She would have had to say something about that or bust, I'm pretty sure. I didn't ask her if she still was going to buy a car, or if she had caved in to Bull about the car money. I thought her taking the taxi home every night was all the answer I needed.

The last day of November I went out to the sand dunes south of Ponte Vedra and set up a handful of flat pint whisky bottles and fired the .45. The dunes were deserted in the rain. I was in a little cup of dunes, hidden from the road, and the sound of the shots carried off across the sand and out to sea. The shots didn't sound anything as loud as the rifles or pistols on an Army firing line. The gun was so heavy it didn't kick much. The short barrel took some getting used to. I used up fifteen rounds out of the fifty in the box and got the hang of loading fresh cartridges in those little half-moon clips.

Anything beyond ten paces, I couldn't hit the bottles, just kicked up sand all around them. If I stood three steps away, they smashed to splinters. The trigger pull was so heavy I had to use two hands to steady the gun. But when I cocked the hammer first it went off almost too easy, before I was ready.

By the time I finished shooting, I had a little quiver in my forearms from the strain, like when I had to do pushups in basic training. Three steps away was good enough. I figured if they were more than three steps away I might could outrun them. I only took seven empty pints out there and when they were busted, I quit. Back at the Chev, I used a yellow pencil stub to push a couple of scraps of cloth from an old T-shirt soaked with ten-in-one oil through the barrel. Then I wiped the whole gun down and wrapped it in the rest of the shirt and put it back under the seat.

I went to play poker the first Friday night in December. I didn't want to, but I hadn't been since that night and I knew I had to go. That was the only way to keep Rennie Cross and Shattuck from getting the idea that

I was ducking them. I don't know why things had to be that way, but that's the way they were.

They already had had too much time to think about how they had been humiliated by a little twerp who was too terrified of them to come back around. If I didn't go where they were soon, they would come after me. I didn't want them to try beating me again. I was through with letting them do that even if they didn't know it. I wasn't going to take it and I didn't have to take it. But I didn't want to go to jail, either.

When I came into the room at Bennett's motel that Friday, I know I was walking tight and funny. There were more poker players there than usual. Enough for two tables. Come to see the fun by God. Even Donlevy was there. That made me feel better right away. He tipped me a wink and brought me a longneck Schlitz from the tub. Such a small thing, but it reminded everybody there of things he didn't need to say.

Neither Rennie Cross nor Shattuck showed up. I didn't have any idea what that meant. But I played poker for four straight hours to make it stick that I wasn't hiding from anybody. I was so concentrated on acting normal that my poker game went completely to hell. I wound up down fifty dollars that I couldn't afford to waste that way. Guys in the game seemed to mention Rennie Cross or Shattuck in every conversation throughout the evening, watching me sideways, always hinting that one of them might show up at any minute. Donlevy just played his usual steady game and kept his mouth shut and smiled a lot. I could smell a whiff of Mary Jane in his pipe smoke. For a careful man, he was careless that way sometimes.

It was after three in the morning before somebody let it slip that Shattuck was working the graveyard shift at the cab company and Rennie Cross was out of town, gone hunting. I played out two more hands and quit. The sons of bitches. They all seemed let down that nothing was going to happen. They all wanted Mrs. Valland's Roman holiday, all right.

Donlevy was a pretty good winner that night. He got the best part of my money on several hands where I tried to bluff him, so that old Colt ended up costing me closer to a hundred bucks than fifty by the time the night was over.

Chapter Twenty-Three

I woke up Saturday morning with sun pouring through the blinds and the phone ringing. It couldn't have been more than nine o'clock.

"I'm not on today, Mabel," I said. "Anyway, it's way too early."

"I ain't working today, either," she said.

I sat straight up in bed. It was Corinne.

"That's right," I said. I sounded like a dope. "You're not, that's right." I still sounded like a dope.

"Sure is a nice day," she said. "After all that rain. December's coming in pretty." She pronounced it purty.

"It's bright all right." I was squinting in the sun and I just couldn't get my mind in gear. I was mumbling.

"You still asleep, Walter?"

"I—no, what makes you think that?"

"Your voice sounds all funny."

"I'm not asleep, though. What's up?"

"I thought it might be nice to go ridin' today," she said.

"You mean now? This morning?"

"Well, it's such a nice day and all. And there ain't nobody home. I was makin' some ice tea and remembered how good you liked Mama's. I make it just as good as she does. I could put some in a Thermos and we could maybe ride down to St. Augustine or something like you've mentioned before."

She sounded like a kid trying to get his big brother to come out and play catch. Like she was afraid I was going to say no.

"Where is everybody?" I said.

"Mama took Ben and Little Luke on the Greyhound up

to Macon since they're out of school a week for Thanksgiving. Daddy's gone fishing down at Cape Canaveral somewhere with Andy Stout and Rennie Cross. You want to go?"

"Let's go," I said. "I've got lots of turkey and stuff. I'll put together some sandwiches. I'll be over as soon as I shower and shave."

"Okay!" She sounded fit to pop.

I must have set some kind of record for getting out of there. The only reason I could throw the food together so fast without spilling it all over everywhere was because I'd been around restaurants so long. I was afraid if I didn't get out of my apartment in a hurry she would call up and change her mind. That would have been too much to take after her calling out of the blue like that. I was cussing myself for staying out late playing poker, and for not getting up early. I never got up early on Saturdays, but that didn't matter right then. I had it bad, all right.

I flooded the Chev getting it started, and cussed myself until it finally turned over. Then I stalled it trying to back out with the engine dead cold. I was in some state. By the time I was rolling, I was sweating like a pig even though it had turned cold enough in the night to drop frost. There still were white patches on the yards where the sun hadn't hit, and car windows on the street were covered with it. Thank God I had parked under the porch. When I turned up the lane, it felt for a minute like I was going into enemy territory. What if Bull had come back for some ungodly reason? But he hadn't.

Corinne was waiting behind the window with the cotton patches in the screen. She came out the minute she saw the car. I had never in my life before had a woman be ready for me when I got there. She had on purple slacks and flat shoes and a man's brown leather bomber jacket over a white blouse, and she had the Thermos jug and a paper sack. She hopped straight in like there were bloodhounds right behind her. I got us out of there and headed south on A1A without saying a word.

Finally I said, "That's some jacket."

"My brother gave it to me," she said. "It's good and warm."

"What made you decide to take off all of a sudden like this?"

"Because I just felt like it. I don't get very many chances just to do something I want to do. Ain't you ever done anything like that?"

"Not for a long time."

"Then it's about time for both of us, ain't it?"

The way she said that really got me. "I'm with you, kid," I said.

"And I'm with you," she said. She sounded happy. "But I ain't no kid."

I had never heard her use that intimate tone of voice, and never thought I would, at least not to me. I immediately got a hard on like a Russian bear and was glad I was wearing my old herringbone jacket, because it was floppy enough to keep me covered.

It's not really that many miles down A1A to St. Augustine, but it almost seemed like a whole day went by on the way. Like slow motion or something. The minute we were south of the Oasis, we were outside anything we had ever done before, and I knew I was going to remember every minute of that drive for the rest of my life. I was partly right. I can remember how the sunlight was, and the crisp way the sea oats stood up on the sand dunes, and the dark shadows under the big oaks behind the dunes. I remember how Corinne looked with her hair tied back loosely, no waitress hairnet, relaxed and laughing, sitting closer to me than she ever had before. Not touching, but close. What I don't remember is a single word we said, or even what we talked about. I remember that we seemed to laugh at just about anything and that I was really honest-to-god happy.

The ocean wind molds all the trees on the ocean side of the highway until they curve the same way the dunes lie. It was so clear that day you could see in under the palmetto scrub and the twisted little oaks that had tried to move out onto the sand. The ocean was flat calm, and had a lot of green in with the blue, and there wasn't a single wisp of cloud in the sky. We passed a pickup truck towing an airboat like they use in the Everglades. There was a Black Labrador retriever in the back of the pickup with a pile of duck decoys and he looked so sad we laughed at him too. It wasn't the kind of day for ducks to behave to suit a Lab.

When we came in across the North River bridge, St. Augustine looked like some kind of magic kingdom out across the marsh. The billboards say it's the oldest town in America, with the oldest store, the oldest schoolhouse, the oldest jail and a real-life Fountain of Youth, discovered in 1513 by Ponce De Leon. It had a wax museum, surrey rides, Ripley's Believe it Or Not and other sure-fire tourist traps.

The first thing she said when we came past the orange and grapefruit stands at the edge of town was that she wanted to go to the fort.

"You ever been to the fort?" I asked.

"No. Just rode by it. Daddy never wanted to go in."

"Let's go then."

We drove into the parking lot down below the fort. There were cars from all over the country. Corinne wanted to count how many different license plates we could see, just like a kid. So we drove all the way through the lot and back again, and she counted twelve different states and Quebec. She didn't even know what a Quebec was, or how a Ford station wagon could be from there. The winter tourists were on the move all right. Some of the cars still were thick with muddy scunge high up along their sides.

"Wonder where they got all that mud?" she wanted to know.

"Snow," I said. "They've been driving through snow. Dirty snow on the road does that."

"I've never even *seen* snow," she said. "Not even in Georgia."

Somehow her saying that made me feel like a real world-traveler. I had seen Ohio snow, Pennsylvania snow, hell, I had even seen German snow.

We parked and went on up to the fort. It sits on a low hill guarding the bay. The Spanish built it when they still had plans to hang onto Florida and got tired of guys like Sir Francis Drake sailing in and burning the town. The walls are coquina and thick as hell. It never lost a garrison except by treaty. We took the tour, and Corinne thought it was awful about the dungeons where the U.S. government had put some tough-guy Indians from the Southwest to cool off. She thought it was wonderful that some of them had starved themselves skinny enough to slip through the gun-slit windows and escape.

She got really interested when the tour guide told us that General Oglethorpe and his Georgians had put it under siege. Corinne didn't think Oglethorpe should have sent his army home to tend their crops instead of going ahead and taking the fort. No matter who else had tried it and failed, she knew Georgians could have done it. Considering Bull Valland and her gun moll mother, and Corinne for that matter, I didn't doubt it for a minute.

From up on the walls we could see the big arm of land that the locals call Anastasia Island off across the bay, and the white flash of surf breaking out past it.

"We almost bought a house over there instead of on

the Beaches," Corinne said.

"The state has a lot of that land on the ocean side," I said. "They have picnic tables and stuff over there. Want to go over there and eat?"

"Okay, if it's not as cold as it is up here."

She was shivering in the light breeze off the bay, even in her bomber jacket. The breeze was cold enough to make your eyes water if you looked right into it. After a minute or two your could lick your lips and taste salt.

"The weather's not that cold," I said. "Look at all those tourists in Bermuda shorts."

"Them are Yankees. That's all right for Yankees, but I'm cold as hell."

"Okay, we'll find a place out of the wind," I said.

"I got to have me some coffee, too. You and your iced tea in December. Jesus!"

Chapter Twenty-Four

We drove across the Bridge of Lions and got Corinne's coffee at an orange juice stand on the highway in front of the Alligator Farm. The state park was almost deserted. There was one big silver Airstream trailer hooked up to a blue Dodge station wagon, parked under the trees at the far end on the parking lot. An old couple sat outside in side-by-side lawn chairs. They had an old army blanket over their laps and were sharing a pair of field glasses like they were at a football game. Three dune buggies were down on the beach, lined up close to the water. Three men and two women in heavy jackets and chest waders stood in the surf, slamming big heavy surf rods out over the breakers. The old couple was watching them fish.

I parked as far away from the old couple as I could get. We sat on top of one of the picnic tables and ate my turkey sandwiches and cold dressing. The iced tea tasted funny out of a Thermos on a cold day, but I drank it all. Corinne's coffee probably smelled a lot better than it tasted. The ocean made that steady rushing sound like breathing that it makes in cool weather. We saw one of the women's surf rods bend way over and start jumping around. She had quite a time before she got what looked like a big channel bass up to the shallows where one of the men gaffed it.

Corinne asked if I liked to go fishing. I told her about when I was a kid fishing for smallmouths in the stream near home, but said it just seemed like too much trouble and expense to go fishing anymore. I told her the last time I went fishing was at Passa Grille south of Saint Pete.

Turned out the Vallands had been to Saint Pete for a

vacation before they moved to the Beaches. We got into a do-you-remember conversation. She asked me if I remembered Webb's City and I told her Webb's City was a Saint Pete landmark. I used to buy groceries from the delicatessen on the ground floor next to the bakery and the fish market. She told me Saint Pete's suburban streets were paved with bricks from a mill in Augusta, Georgia where her grandfather had worked. I remembered the brick streets and she said every single brick had "Augusta" stamped on them. I didn't remember that.

Corinne remembered the municipal dock near the big Sorena Hotel, a place I used to know all the cooks from. She had a picture in her wallet of Ben and Little Luke when they were really young, squinting on the dock with the bright sails of the little Sunfish sailboats there in the background. Both of them had on little scaled-down captain's hats like charterboat skippers wore and that tourists bought on the boardwalk.

Being Corinne, she had some strong opinions about south Florida. She didn't like Gulf Beach sand. She said it was too mushy and reminded her of Georgia quicksand instead of the hard dry sand of Jacksonville Beach. We both remembered the sponge boats at Tarpon Springs where a hard-hat diver would go down to show tourists how sponge fishing was done before plastic ruined the market. She said that young Ben had been terrified the whole time they were out on the sponge boat because he had seen a movie where the diver's hose was cut.

It was all just ordinary conversation, nothing special, except the feeling of being with Corinne on something like a real date. That day just seemed to last and last. I know they say that time flies when you are having fun. And I know time drags on slow night shifts and waiting at the dentist and serving hard time, which is the opposite of enjoyment. What I had forgotten, or never known until that day in St. Augustine, was that time stands still when you are happy.

After we finished the leftovers we walked down the beach a little, but Corinne got chilled again so we went back and sat in the car with the heater running. We watched the pelicans on patrol, and the sandpipers working the edge of the tide. One of the dune buggies left, lunging over the sand like a boat on water. The retired couple went inside their Airstream and the rest of the fishermen climbed inside an old milk truck with sawed-out fenders and fat tires that they had converted into a camper. Smoke started trickling out of a little stovepipe on the roof, and it looked cozy.

I remember thinking that the retired couple with the trailer looked so at peace together, like their life's race was run and they'd won. They looked maybe twenty years older than me. I wondered what it would be like to make it to retirement age as a couple at peace with each other, and felt a little bittersweet shadow cross my perfect day, as if I knew that wasn't ever going to happen for me. Then I forced myself to stop thinking like that so I could enjoy what time I had left with Corinne.

After a while we stopped talking and just sat there. I didn't know what was going to happen next. I was afraid that it was almost time for her to come to her senses and tell me she had to get home right now.

I could feel her there next to me like a magnet. I was afraid to turn and look at her because I wanted to touch her so bad. But I was afraid to. I was afraid one touch would bring the whole day down with a crash. I never was the kind of man who was confident about when to make a move on a woman and I never had a lot of practice before I got married. I knew what to do once that awkwardness was out of the way. That wasn't the problem. I never had any complaints there. It was just screwing up my courage to reach out and start it that I didn't know how to do.

I just couldn't think the thing through with Corinne. If I tried something and botched it, it would ruin this day for me. I would lose all this I already had, starting with the fact she had called me up out of the blue and had made iced tea just for me. If that was all I was ever going to have with her, I wanted to have it clean, so the memory would always be complete and happy. More than once in my life I was pretty sure that I had let the right moment with a woman go by for lack of knowing how to start something. It looked like this was going to be more of the same. I just couldn't risk messing up this nice day. It was like I'd been struck dumb.

She finally got a pack of cigarettes out of her bomber jacket and tapped one into her hand. I reached to light it with my old Zippo, that I used to use Army diesel fuel in in Germany, and the damn wick flared up. She jerked back and dropped the cigarette. I jerked back and dropped the lighter. I had to fumble around on the floorboards to find it and put out the flame. I asked her if she was all right.

"It singed my lips," she said.

Before I could think I said, "Well, I only know one way to fix that."

She looked at me. "You mean kiss it and make it well?"

I couldn't speak. I just nodded. She twisted her body and leaned toward me and I saw her lips part and the tip of her tongue come up between them. Her eyes were closing and it was just like in the movies, except for the tongue.

When her tongue slid across mine, right away, no hesitation, it was like getting electrocuted. I came on hard like a light switch going on and she just kept leaning into me, kissing me, her left breast a warm solid weight against the side of my chest. When we finally pulled apart, she didn't move six inches away, and now her eyes were half-open and kind of smoky.

I *said*, "My god!" It came out hoarse.

"I thought you never were going to get around to that," she said, real soft. The Georgia accent was thicker than usual.

"I've wanted to, for a long time."

"Since the first?"

I couldn't lie, not with her looking at me like that. "Not at first. I just liked you, and liked riding around with you at first."

"You never once tried anything. You telling the truth now?" It was the first time I had ever heard her sound uncertain about anything.

"I don't know when I started wanting to," I said. "I was just so afraid it might mess things up to try something. You'd just think I was like those others..."

"You're not anything like those others," she said. "Come here. Let's try that again."

I felt myself blush. I mean really blush. The blood was so hot in my face it felt like it must be glowing like a sunset. She smiled and touched the side of my face with her palm. I turned and kissed her palm, and she put the other hand up and turned my face and kissed me, leaning into me hard now. I lost all track of time.

When we pulled apart again, and again not very far apart, things were different. She had a faraway look in her eyes and her breathing was different. So was mine for that matter. My heart was beating so hard I thought I was going to rattle apart. I had one hand inside her bomber jacket against the side of her breast, and my thumb was making gentle little circles against the slipperiness of her blouse. I could feel the bump of her nipple through the cloth. A little shudder went through her and she put her hand on mine, pressing it into her, hard.

Somehow the sun was on the horizon. Lights were on

in the Airstream trailer and in the camper down on the beach. The wind was picking up. Her face was in shadow when I kissed her again.

"Ohhh, Walter," she said in a sleepy voice. "What do we do now?

I could hardly speak. "I suppose it wouldn't be romantic to say let's go to a motel, would it?"

She pressed my hand hard into her again and kissed the side of my mouth. "What's not romantic?" she whispered. "I don't have to be home until tomorrow morning..."

Chapter Twenty-Five

*B*ack in Saint Augustine I checked us into one of those all-brick Spanish motor courts on the bayfront overlooking the Bridge of Lions built around a central court full of cabbage palms and Spanish bayonet. I would have liked something really posh like the Hotel Ponce De Leon, but I didn't have enough money with me. I had to keep glancing out the office window when I signed in, to convince myself Corinne really was in the Chev.

I followed her up the outside iron stairs to the second floor and fitted the room key in the door. She was quiet, carrying her little paper bag. I thought she was carrying the bag because she thought she should have some kind of luggage, which meant she had been planning ahead. My heart just turned over at that thought.

When we were inside with the shades drawn, I took her in my arms, nervous because we hadn't touched since I came out of the office. Then she kissed me back and it was all right again. I had both arms under her leather jacket now, holding her against me, and she slipped a knee between my legs. Then she put both hands on my chest and pushed me back slightly. We hadn't turned on the light and I couldn't see her eyes.

"I have to use the ladies'," she said, real quiet. "You get in bed and start getting it warm."

I stood there until the bathroom light came on. I felt like a kid on his first heavy date. I couldn't really believe this was happening. I checked to make sure the door was chained, and took off my tweed jacket. I heard water running, and went over to the bed and turned the covers down. I stripped down to my shorts and got between the covers. The sheets were cold. The only light in the room came from around the bathroom door and a faint blue glow on the curtains from the neon outside. Footsteps walked by on the breezeway outside. I lost my erection as soon as I got between the sheets, hearing strange footsteps so close. She seemed to be taking a long time in there. Maybe she had changed her mind. Maybe I had just thought she wanted me to undress. What if she walked out fully dressed with me laying there in my boxer shorts under the covers like a damned fool?

The light went out and the door opened, and she came quickly toward the bed. I vaguely saw her form stoop and drop something by the bed and heard the creak of leather. Her jacket. Then the bed sagged and she was there, slipping under the covers naked and into my arms so fast it took my breath away. Her hands on my back were cold, but her body was burning up.

"Hold me tight," she said. "I need to get warm."

Her back under my fingertips was soft and sleek. I had never felt skin that smooth and fine. My fingertips traced the slight indentations where her bra had been. I kissed her, and ran my hands down her side, cupping her butt. Even her ass was smooth as satin under my fingers.

"Why've you got your underpants on?" she said.

"I'll take 'em off," I said. I did, and she came back into my arms. "My god, you're so soft," I said into her mouth.

I reached between her legs and she made a pleased little sound in her throat. She was dry at first, but slicked up right away when I ran my thumb up and down through the coarse hair, finding the path to her bud. I took it between my thumb and finger, and she shoved up against me, her arms tight around my neck. I began a slow rhythm, and she matched it with her hips. She let go my neck with one hand to reach between us. As soon as she touched me there I started getting hard again, and slippery. She made a quiet chuckling sound.

"I saw that damp spot on your pants when you came out of the office," she said.

I sped up the motion of my hand.

"My god, Walter," she said. "Put your finger in me. I can come to your finger."

I put two fingers into her, and left my thumb where it had been, and she began to breathe in long shuddering gasps. Then she was there. She dug her heels in and held herself up against me, groaning. I put my free hand against her mouth and she bit down on the heel of my hand, hard. Then she pulled me down and kissed me over and over again, as she calmed down. She was stroking me steadily with the other hand.

"Easy," I said. My voice sounded choked. "I'm too close..."

"Have you got a rubber?" she whispered. "Hurry! I've gotta have it!" She felt me tense up. "What's wrong?"

I buried my face in her hair. "Stupid. Stupid. No, I never thought..."

"It's all right." She let go of me and reached up to pat me on the shoulder. "It's all right." She pulled away and sat up on the edge of the bed. Cold air hit my sweating body and I thought I was going to be sick.

"Corinne...?"

She was leaning over, fumbling with her jacket. I could hear the leather creaking again. Then she turned back. "If you say one word, or even think it, I'll wring your scrawny neck!" she said fiercely. "Here, scootch over here to me. I've got one."

I did what she said, and her hands were on me. "Uh-oh! What happened here?"

"I'm sorry, " I said. "I just—it just..."

"Shh-h!" She half-giggled. "You're really something, Walter. Nice Walter, who never even thought—H'mm."

She bent over me, and her hair brushed lightly across my belly. My stomach muscles jumped and fluttered. I felt her warm moist breath on me.

"My god, Corinne."

I threw my head back. Sweat was turning cold on my chest but I could feel the heavy push of her breasts against my thighs and then the hot pressure of her mouth on me, and if I had a heart attack and died right there, it would have been all right with me.

I could feel the slipperiness of her tongue on me, and then cold air as her mouth lifted and her hands fumbled with me.

"That's more like it," she said, and I felt the pressure of the rubber as she snuggled it over me. "Push back up the bed," she said. "Hurry!"

She crawled up after me and astraddle me. I went into her snug, right up to the hilt. She put her hands on my shoulders and leaned down and kissed me lightly. I tasted myself on her lips.

"Right there," she said, and reared back and started to move, slowly at first but gathering speed. The bedsprings began to squeak quietly. I cupped her breasts, and her nipples nudged into my palms when she leaned down. Then we were into it, locked into it, and I wasn't going to last, couldn't last, but she was already there and then I was, too, right behind her, and hung on for dear life while white-hot flashes went off behind my eyes and I exploded like I was never going to stop.

We lay like that for a long time, her on top. I could feel her heart begin to slow down where it was knocking against my ribs, and my pulse gradually stopped roaring in my ears. Our bodies were slippery with sweat. I reached under her elbows and pulled her up gently. She made a little protesting sound when I fell out of her, but I eased her up until she could straighten her legs and snuggle up in the crook of my arm.

"Whew!" I said, stroking her face.

"M'mmm." She burrowed her nose down against my neck. "God, it's been so *long* since I was wrapped all around a man."

I was so happy I felt like crying. Just the sleek feel of her body all along me, and the weight of her on my arm made me feel like everything in the world was okay. I couldn't remember the last time I had been with a woman other than Chris. Really been with one. We had gradually stopped doing anything before the TB took over completely, because, she was so tired and wrung out most of the time. There was one woman that Donlevy tried to fix me up with out at the Below The Border before I went to work for Dawson's. We ended up trying to do something in the back seat of the Chev, but I never was acrobatic enough for that. It hadn't worked out very well and I had never seen her again, or wanted to. I didn't want to think about that now. I just wanted to be right here, where I was, and forget everything.

"You dozin' off, Walter?" Corinne said quietly.

"Just trying to recover. I'm way past forty, Corinne."

"Huh! Couldn't prove it by me."

I kissed her forehead. She reached up and kissed me on the lips. I kissed her back, and that went on for a while. I was amazed to feel myself beginning to come back to life against her hip. She felt it too, and broke the kiss.

"I think we got a problem, Walter."

"Call that a problem? At my age I call that a blessing." I was stroking the side of her breast, up to the nipple. I couldn't get enough of that satin flesh. I never knew human flesh could be so smooth to the touch.

"That's not what I mean, smarty pants. You don't think I carry a dozen damn rubbers with me everywhere I go, do you?"

"I thought I wasn't saying anything about what you were carrying or you'd wring my scrawny neck," I said.

"M'mm." She nuzzled me under the chin. "Not *so* scrawny up close. Quit that!" She grabbed my wrist where I had reached to dip a finger into her again.

"What? This?"

"God!" she said. Just like that she was into it again, humping against my hand. She was there even quicker this time. I felt pretty smug.

"What're we gonna *do*?" she whispered, touching me. She sounded like she was half-moaning.

"Just keep doing that," I said, and my voice caught. "Do it harder."

"Like this?" She leaned up on one elbow to get a better grip. "Like this?"

"Just like that," I said. "Just like that. Just like that."

Then I couldn't say anything or do anything but just hung on tried to keep from yelling out loud when she finished me off.

"I've never done that to anybody before," she said. "Was it all right?"

"It was fine." I shivered. "God!"

"Seems like a waste of a good hard-on, though."

I couldn't help laughing at her. Anything she said made me happy. "Such language. You got any better ideas?"

"We've got all night, don't forget. It's early yet. You hungry?"

"No."

"You will be. I am, already. Let's get dressed and go get something to eat. And I bet even St. Augustine has a drug store."

"A drug store?"

She punched me in the arm. "Don't be dense, dummy. I ain't through with you yet."

She wasn't either, not by a Georgia mile.

Chapter Twenty-Six

We had early breakfast at Below the Border and I couldn't stop grinning at her. She was smiling and relaxed like I'd never seen her before but it all seemed perfectly normal that morning. Donlevy wasn't on shift so I didn't have to worry about him making smart remarks. Ronnie was behind the counter. Ronnie was always behind the counter it seemed. But even Ronnie was full of surprises: he trotted out a kind of charm that would have done the Italian counts he claimed as ancestors right proud. He deferred to Corinne like a princess without a hint of making fun behind his nasal drip. It was pretty clear he liked her, and for whatever reason he had always liked me. He wouldn't even let me pay for breakfast, a first.

It wasn't until we hit the Oasis on A1A going north that Corinne began to kind of drift back away from me across the car seat, and inside herself. I was sorry to see it, but it made sense. People had been thinking this of us all damn fall, and now here it was, and us riding around in each other's laps would just nail it down for keeps. From time to time she'd reach over below the line of the windows and pat me on the thigh, just a little reassuring tap or two. She didn't have her Indian face on yet, but you would never have known she was doing that I you saw us from another car. When we came level with Dawson's she got completely still.

"Don't turn up the lane when we get there," she said, real quiet. "Just drop me at the corner and keep driving. None of this is anybody's business but ours, okay?"

I said okay and when I stopped the car she was out of there and gone up the lane so fast she was out of sight before I got in gear.

I didn't have to go to work until Tuesday, and nothing else was pressing to do. I just drove around in circles for a while and tried to get my mind around how things had changed for sure now. I must have swung by the foot of her lane five times over the next couple of hours, for what reason I couldn't say. To prove to myself there really was a house there with toy arrow holes in the screens, and that she lived there? Wondering if her family got home before she got home or were still gone? Hoping to get another glimpse of her? What if everybody had stayed gone longer than they thought and she was free as I was for the rest of the day?

What would we do if she was? We couldn't go to my place, it would be too easy to be spotted.

Too many people were out and about that morning, and who knew how many of them knew us from the restaurant. I decided not to press my luck and just went home. I was all the way inside before I worried that maybe she had been alone at home this whole time and tried to call me. But for some reason what we'd just had made me sure that hadn't happened, and I didn't get all worried.

So I didn't call. I didn't want to risk stirring up any bad luck that morning. I hadn't had that many times in my life where I felt that good and peaceful, and I just kind of floated through the day in a cloud. I cleaned out the apartment, which needed doing and gave me something to do. Then I took my piled up dirty clothes to the Laundromat and put the Chev in the seven-day service station for an oil change while I washed everything. By the end of the day I felt just right about not calling Corinne or trying to stretch things. I didn't have to. I felt like I was all set for the rest of my life, and everything was going to come out fine.

I didn't really know what I meant by everything

coming out fine, which is probably just as well. Things already had begun to go sour and I didn't even know it.

But everything on the Beaches seemed bright and clean and fresh washed after all the rain, and I thought it was the finest winter I had ever seen. I even caught myself humming music a time or two, and I hadn't done that since Chris and I were courting. I pretty much kept to myself and enjoyed the company.

Tuesday at two, when I pulled into the side lot at Dawson's there was a taxi waiting by the takeout door. I saw the number eight on the roof light and started to tighten up. Then I saw it wasn't Shattuck driving, but the day man, Shipwreck. The story was Shipwreck was a naval officer who got some trouble drinking and wound up on the beach, as they say in Navy jargon. These particular Beaches had a name for everything, so Shipwreck he became. I'd never heard anybody call him anything else.

I nodded to him as I walked across the lot and he nodded back. A waitress came out the take-out door. It was Alberta, a tall thin blonde who was always chewing gum at a mile a minute or trying to smoke a cigarette sexy like Lauren Bacall. She wasn't doing either one right now.

She had on a sweater pulled tight around her. She went toward the cab slow and bent over, like an old woman. Her eyes were puffy and her mascara had run. She was crying and her nose was all pink and bloated up. She had a handkerchief up there, and there were bright red splotches on it too, like a nosebleed. Shipwreck hopped out and came around to open the door for her.

"You hurt yourself?" I said.

She turned on me a lot faster than it seemed she could have moved a minute before.

"You!" she shouted. Honked, rather. Sound was having a hard time with that nose. A little red bubble dribbled onto her lips.

"Hell—your nose is bleeding," Shipwreck said. He took her elbow. "C'mon, sit down quick and lean your head back..."

She snatched away from him, still glaring at me. "You teach that bitch manners!" she squawked at me. "You better, if you know what's good for you."

"What the hell are you talking about?"

"That crummy little Georgia whore you like so good, you sorry prick! That's who I'm talking about!"

She dabbled at the blood and cried some more.

"Corinne did that?" Shipwreck looked astonished. "I don't believe it!"

"What do you know, you idiot?" She sat down in the cab. "Oh, what's the use? Men! Jesus, Jesus. What is it--is her pussy covered with jools or something?"

"You shut your mouth," I said.

She jerked her head up. "Well is it? Is it?"

"Shut your filthy mouth," I said.

"You can't threaten me, you prick! Bob Hoolian will fix you, you sorry prick! He'll fix you good, you watch!"

Hoolian was a Duval County deputy sheriff Alberta had been shacking up with that summer.

"We better go now, honey," Shipwreck put in. "The meter's running." He sounded worried.

"I'm going," she said. "Don't you put on airs either, you wrinkled old Navy fart! I know all about you too, don't think I don't. Men! Jesus!"

I walked away before she could start in again. It looked like one of Corinne's arguments she was always having had gotten out of hand. That's what I was thinking. I still didn't see it coming.

Dawson and Corinne were standing in the walkway between the take-out and the kitchen. He was saying something that sounded mad in a hoarse whisper. Corinne was looking at him like Crazy Horse must have looked at

Custer. If I was Dawson I would have backed off a little. Dawson saw me come in.

"You!" he said.

"It's me, all right," I said. I grinned at him. I couldn't help it, because she was standing right there and I had to grin at somebody. "That makes two people in a row surprised as hell to see me today."

"Come to my office!" He turned and started off. "You too, Corinne," he said back over his shoulder.

He didn't need to add that. She was right after him like a bat out of hell. She was smoking mad, all right. I had never seen her this mad. I followed them, but I just couldn't take it in. If any of this had been going on when Mabel called she had kept it to herself, which meant it had started since. She would have had to spill gossip about a catfight or pop a button.

We got inside his office and Dawson told me to close the door. Almost before it clicked, he was shouting.

"I don't give a good god damn if you two go balling up one side of this state and down the other, you keep it to yourselves and out of my god damn restaurant, you hear me? I don't need no goddamn screaming and hair pulling on the floor. I'm running a restaurant here, not a god damn cat house—you sit back down!"

Corinne had parked as soon as we came in, but now she was up and starting toward his desk.

"You watch your language," she said. She was talking in a dead calm voice. "You just keep your voice down and watch your foul mouth." The Georgia accent was so thick you could slice it. "If you can't behave in a civil manner, I will shove my fist down your throat. If I can't do it, I've got brothers in Georgia who can and will. I don't know just who exactly you think you are, but *nobody* talks to a Valland like that."

Dawson just goggled. I thought he was either going to

have a stroke or bust a gut. Before he could do either, I thought I better say something.

"We might as well of stayed outside if we are going to get screamed at," I said. My hands were icy cold and my voice sounded like somebody else's. I saw it coming now, all right. Oh, I saw it all right. But he had to say it. He had to say it to me. "Would you like to start over and tell me what the hell is going on?"

It seemed to take him a long time to come out of it. Finally he didn't seem about to bust anymore. He seemed to unswell slowly, like the air going out of a beach ball.

"All right," he said. "You two were seen together in St. Augustine. Coming out of a motel for God's sake! I warned you about this once, Walter."

I couldn't look at Corinne. I couldn't stand her knowing we had discussed her like a piece of meat. Here it was, all right. I couldn't believe his righteous tone of voice. He sounded like some kind of crazy Holy Roller preacher.

"Well?" he said, in the same tone. Now I was cold everywhere except my head, where it felt like I had a fever.

"Me and Alberta was arguing," Corinne said off to the side. Her voice seemed to come across a big space. "That dumbbell, she don't know nothing about raising kids. Nothin! I told her, too, and then she said...what she said...and I just let her have it, right in the nose. She just fell down and started to squall like stuck pig."

"All she said was a proper mother wouldn't be off running around with a married..." Dawson started.

Corinne glared at him and he shut up. Okay, that explained why Alberta lit into me like she did. She was stupider than I ever thought, to say something like that to Corinne's face. It was a wonder they hadn't had to call an ambulance, not a cab.

Nobody better ever question Corinne about the kind of mother she was, not ever. I thought anybody would have had sense enough to know that.

I kept thinking I should have known, should have known, over and over. It just isn't in the cards to be happy, not even for one day. One lousy day, and now this, making dirty foot tracks all over what we'd had. It must be like when you step on a land mine in wartime. I was all blasted apart and knew it, but I couldn't feel the pain yet. I was numb all over, like the circulation had been cut off all at once.

Dawson ignored Corinne, staring right at me. "Well?" he said again, in that Sunday damnation voice, like he had a right to speak to me like that.

I started walking toward his desk. I felt like I was walking on twenty-foot stilts in slow motion. I saw my hand go out like a boom on a big crane, way below my eyes, and pick up his telephone.

"What the hell do you think you're doing?" Dawson said.

I dialed a number and a woman's voice said, "Below the Border."

"Angie? This is Walter," I said. "Tell Ronnie that Dawson has just fired me, and I will be out to talk to him about that job he's always promising me." I hung up before she could react.

Dawson was looking at me like I was crazy. "What did you do that for?"

I leaned on the phone. "You just fired me. But you didn't fire Corinne, and you're not going to. There's no need, now."

"I—hell, no! I didn't fire you, I'm just warning you one last time not to..."

"Go to hell," I said.

"*What?* What did you say to me?" He was getting loud again.

"Just go to hell," I said.

He was beginning to puff up again.

"You're not gonna draw unemployment off me! I didn't fire you, you ungrateful little prick. You quit! After all I did for you!"

"You self-righteous windbag," I said. "If you ever use that tone of voice to me again, I will blow your god damn brains out. You hear me?"

"I—"

"You hear me?"

"You get the fuck out of here or I'll call the cops!"

"Go fuck yourself," I said, and walked out. I didn't even look at Corinne.

"And stay out!" he screamed. "Stay the hell out of my restaurant from now on."

The early eaters were trying to pretend they couldn't hear anything out of the ordinary going on, and they looked like a pack of fools. To hell with them, too. To hell with the whole god damn world.

Chapter Twenty-Seven

When I got out to the Below the Border, Ronnie said he could only give me the long Sunday day shift and the graveyard on Wednesdays and Thursdays. He said he would have had to fire one of Donlevy's assistants to give me any more than that, and nobody deserved the sack just now. Everybody was working real hard for their Christmas money. In the meantime I could have a numbers run on the Beaches, because he needed somebody who knew the pickups, and who he trusted.

I said okay and he gave me thirty dollars against my first run. It was good to have some money in my pocket, but starting again with the numbers scared me. I didn't want to go to jail.

He told me not to worry, he had just read in the *Times-Union* the other day where the District Attorney said there was no such thing as *bolita* in north Florida. Then he laughed until his jowls shook in that way of his. *Bolita* is what we called the numbers back then and most of it was run out of that restaurant I had started with in Tampa. So I was back in the numbers racket, though I never thought I would be. I had done it to myself too. Dawson's wasn't the first job I quit cold, and some of them even took me back after I cooled off. But I had never threatened to blow anybody's heads off before. Nobody had ever tried to get into my personal business like that before either.

Even now I feel nervous saying much about the *bolita*. Somebody in Tampa told me the name stood for little ball, for the little balls they drew in the Cuban National Lottery. Back then *bolita* was about only gambling ordinary folks could do, and a whole lot of people in North Florida knew the District Attorney was blowing smoke about whether it was there or not. We just wondered if he was stupid, or on the take himself.

As I remember Fidel Castro was still a failed first baseman and practicing dentist when I got to Tampa. By the time I left Saint Pete he was up in the Cuban mountains playing bandit and by 1959 he had marched into Havana. The numbers guys were as worried about what would come next as I guess the stock markets are these days every time some new ayatollah pops up. I think I was in Raiford before it was for sure that Fidel was going Commie, and before he double-crossed the mob by fixing the *bolita* numbers so that whole books got cleaned out. Mrs. Valland would have said it always made the devil laugh to see a bitter bit.

A whole lot of Americans bet a whole lot of money on what numbers would be on those little balls when they were cut out of the cloth. On the Beaches, customers would stop by some place like Mac's Pool Hall on Jacksonville Beach and hand over a dollar with their bet. One of my pickups was a Negro maid who worked one the fancy homes in Ponte Vedra, and siphoned all the rich folks bets from the yardmen and drivers and cooks. The rich people weren't too rich to play too; they just did it from the comfort of home.

My job was just like running a trap line, which I did one winter as a kid in Ohio. Bought a new bicycle that spring with pelt money too, but that's another story.

You'd go to each pickup point and they'd hand you over the little slips of paper with the numbers on them, and the cash. If the cops got you while you were holding the slips of paper and the money, they'd lean on you hard to try to find out who you were taking it to. *Bolita* gave cops something to do that was more interesting than writing traffic tickets or trying to keep husbands from killing their wives. Billy Jarvis told me that *bolita* was the most fun cops had since Prohibition was repealed and the rumrunners went away and the only illegal liquor left to bother about was homegrown moonshine.

It was years later in Raiford that I read where a lot of states had got into the legal lottery business. Now the states were raking it in off the top, gambling didn't seem to be so awful anymore. Right about that same time Raiford started filling up with small-time dope pushers. A lot of the old Prohibition cops had switched to drugs about the same time the mob did, but at least as far as I could see they really got going after they lost gambling as a hobby. The cops had them a new crusade to keep from being bored waiting for real crime to occur.

When Ronnie got me back into the *bolita* the idea of a legal lottery would have been like something on the *Twilight Zone* on television. The cops acted dead serious about keeping anybody from playing the numbers. They claimed the numbers financed everything else. I didn't know, and didn't want to know. I'd turn my numbers and cash in to the squirrely little bookkeeper in her nest behind Ronnie's cash register and my part was done. She'd count the cash and I'd get a percentage for all I collected. A commission, basically. That was for the risk of running the numbers in. I don't even know how they kept track of who won and how to pay the winners. The less I knew the better. I took the cash out for any winners on my next run. The biggest winners on my run caught a thousand-dollar combination once in a while. There were enough fifty- and hundred-dollar winners to keep plenty of people putting up their bucks.

Mac, who ran the pool hall, was glad to see me back on the run. The Jacksonville owner of the hall paid him minimum wage. He made a living by fishing the sailors at nine-ball who thought they had learned to shoot pool in Philly or L.A., but the *bolita* was his recreation.

"It's better than going to a movie," he told me. "I ain't much of a reader so I don't spend money on books. You ought to try it, Walter. That dollar gives me recreation all week long. As long as I've got a dollar down, I'm a player, get it? I'm in on things. Lightning might strike. It has before. Even if it don't, where else can you spend a dollar and get that much excitement for your money?"

The ratty old envelope he handed me was stuffed. Must have been over two hundred dollars in there. That meant about twenty for me. Maybe some of the sailors were trying to make their paychecks back after playing nine-ball with Mac. The return address said *Veteran's Administration.*

"I didn't know you were a veteran," I said.

"Walter, there's probably a library full of stuff you don't know. Everybody on these Beaches has got a life story to tell, but nobody wants to listen, nobody cares. We just mind our own business, just like you."

By the time I picked up from the Ponte Vedra maid I must have had close to a thousand dollars in the car. That more than covered the thirty advance, and looked like I might have some money for Christmas if I was careful. I dropped it off at Below the Border and drove on into Jacksonville to sign up for unemployment. I didn't think Dawson would fight the claim despite what he said, and even if he did, he'd probably lose. I had the history of him closing and laying people off every winter to back me up. They probably wouldn't even ask him.

It was nice to have the thirty dollars in my pocket, and more coming, but it made me nervous as hell to be out of steady work. I kept thinking about the fifty dollars I had blown on poker to show I wasn't afraid of Shattuck, and the fifty I had spent on the gun because I was. There's no point worrying after gone money, but I couldn't help think I would have had almost two hundred dollars I could count on. If the unemployment came through that would sure help.

I made it to the state office just before closing, and told my story to a bored flat-faced woman. She could have cared less about a slob cook, now she was one of the office class. She kept looking at the clock like she was afraid I would make her late to punch out. She got it all down, though, and sent me upstairs to where another bunch of clerks had files of where jobs could be had. That part was already closed so I'd have to come back.

On my way out of the building I nearly got run over by the office class. They were all lining up by the time clock with their cards, thump-chugging it without even looking. I went out with the crowd. They were all dressed up like they were going to church. I felt like a bum in my cook's whites, and being out of a job made it worse. I just felt useless and in the way of everybody. I took one look at the traffic going by like a millrace, everybody trying to beat each other to the bridges that led to Arlington, Southside and the Beaches, and said to hell with it. I left my car where it was and found a bar in a side street. The drafts were cheap, forty cents a schooner, so I stayed.

I knew tomorrow I would begin to get shook. Maybe Chris' parents would have to take over the payments for the hospital. If I didn't get something more than those few days at the Below the Border I would begin to get scared. People have got to eat, though, and too many people make money out of feeding them for a cook or a waitress to be out of work too long. I could probably be working tomorrow if I tried at the Beaches, but I wanted to get sprung from the Beaches for now. I couldn't afford to move, but at least I could get a job away from there for a while. I thought the *bolita* would pay the rent and the car payment, so I would be okay until the unemployment started.

I knew I couldn't work on the Beaches for a while. I just couldn't. Everybody would be talking about me getting fired because of Corinne, even if it wasn't exactly true. There would be more people like Shattuck and Alberta to start in on me about it. I don't know what makes people think they have that right, but they sure do think so. If you try to tell them it's none of their business they get worse, or get nasty, like Shattuck.

Things just kept going around and around in my mind and I just kept drinking. I didn't dare even think about Corinne. I had to be very careful not to think about her, and that good feeling I'd had the last few days until I drove into the parking lot at Dawson's. I had to hold thinking about Corinne in reserve, because it was going to have to last me a long time now. What we'd had that day and night and morning was mine now and nobody could ever take it away from me if I was careful, and didn't go where they could talk it to death, talk all over it. If I kept it in reserve it would always be mine, like money in the bank.

I couldn't get over Dawson's self-righteousness. Thinking about him made me mad all over. I would never forget that tone in his voice. I never would have thought he was like that. You get where you trust somebody, and they go and pull that. None of it would have happened if somebody hadn't seen us and just had to gossip, but small towns are like that. Dawson didn't have to act that way, but he had, and that was all over now.

The bar I was in was a drab little city bar where everybody knew each other. Probably lived in the neighborhood. They probably had their own gossip right now about somebody they knew. They sat close to each other and talked real loud over the music. The louder they are, the stupider they are. That's something I worked out a long time ago and it never has failed to be true. The women kept playing the jukebox over and over, hillbilly music about every kind of cheating heart there ever was. I never actually hated hillbilly music until that night. I should have got out of there and gone to the Beaches and got settled in a more familiar bar where I had friends but I just kept putting it off and finally somebody turned on the god damned lights and it was closing time. I tried to buy a six-pack from the package store but they wouldn't let me, and said I should have thought of it sooner. Suddenly everybody was a moralist.

I was afraid to drive right away with that much beer in me, so I started walking and looking for a lighted neon sign. A freezing wind was blowing trash through the streets and it was cold as hell, but it couldn't get through the beer. I felt hot and sticky, and was sweating under my arms and in my crotch. I found a Waffle House and started toward it. A city prowl car looked me over, but I saw the right-hand guy notice my whites under my old Army field jacket, and glance up toward Waffle House. He waved, and I waved back.

The woman working the counter had the whole place to herself. I couldn't see back into the kitchen. She said He'p yew? and Thanks when I paid her, and that was all she said. She didn't even glance at me once while I sat there. She poured coffee refills by remote control. She had that thousand-mile stare, like she lived alone on a desert island and never saw a soul. A city at night is farther away from everybody else than they even make islands, anymore. I remembered those eyes. She was right where she wanted to be, and nobody else in the world even existed. I didn't exist, sitting right there.

The grill was dirty. The breakfast steak had that rancid taste from a dirty grill, and the home fries were half-raw. Whoever was back there was some cook all right. The coffee was worse. I shoveled it all in, though, to soak up some of that cheap beer. I was getting a hell of a headache now, and I knew when I left the beer wouldn't protect me from the cold anymore. I hated the idea of the long drive home on the empty highway, but there wasn't another place in the world I could go. I was beginning to want sleep real bad, and was afraid I would doze off and wreck the Chev if I didn't get home pretty quick. I would have stayed in the Waffle House long enough to sober up, but the dirty grill and raw potatoes finished any thought of that.

It seemed like the final lousy trick of the day, for me to end up eating off somebody else's dirty goddamn grill.

Chapter Twenty-Eight

The weather continued cold. I worked my first Wednesday and Thursday graveyards at Ronnie's and then took a package of winnings with me to distribute at Mac's and the other Beaches stops. Dawson's looked remote and strange when I drove by, as if I had never worked there. My fuel oil in the apartment was running low and I was trying to save most of my *bolita* commissions for Christmas. I bundled up in all the quilts on the bed and slept cold. It wasn't bad except the time between getting up to get in the shower. The coldest night, I used Chris' old enema bag for a hot water bottle.

I used a lot of hot water every time I took a shower just to soak the chill out. Enough electricity to run a water heater was still affordable back then. That old garage apartment was built for summer vacationers, not winter residents. I wished I had got the landlady to move at least one of the old junkers so I could put the Chev inside. But I always had enough antifreeze put in for an Ohio winter, a habit I never kicked even in St. Pete, so the Chev worked better than I did. That first midweek graveyard shift at the Below the Border got my sleep pattern way out of sync. I took to driving around the Beaches for hours before I went to work, the hours I would have normally been cooking at Dawson's.By the time I got back to the apartment at daylight after the graveyard shift I could finally sleep.

On the nights I wasn't working, I still found it impossible to just sit in the apartment. The Chev heater was better than the Duotherm anyway. I didn't shave between the days I worked at Ronnie's. When I did shave, my face got raw from a dull razor. I kept forgetting to buy a new package of blades. I told Chris' folks I was unlikely to find anything steady until after Christmas but that I had some money saved aside, which was a lie to cover the bolita money. They hadn't really believed Dawson's winter experiment would pan out, so I just let them think that it hadn't, and that was why I wasn't working.

Sometimes while I drove around at night I would try to think of a Christmas present for Chris, and just couldn't. It was like she wasn't really there anymore. I always had a hard time thinking about people much when they were away. Out of sight out of mind, I guess. I never sent a Christmas card or birthday card or anything like that unless Christine nagged me to do it. Now there was nobody to remind me, and no one that mattered but her and Sally and her folks. Getting money orders mailed regularly for the TB and for Sally, and planning to go over there for visits, took up so much of my thinking that cards for them seemed pointless. But I was planning to go over there for Christmas, so I was thinking about presents. Sally mailed me notes on drawing paper with flowers and birds drawn on them in crayon. It seemed like I had always got them, thanks to her grandmother. But I never sent her anything back.

Chris' mother sent a note every other week or so to report on Chris and to say how well Sally was doing in school. She always said Chris was too tired to write, and it always sounded like she was making excuses. I don't know what she thought about me not writing back. Maybe she made excuses for me to Christine and Sally. She was that kind of woman, always trying to smooth things over. If I had something to tell Sally or her grandparents, I called long-distance from a phone booth so they'd keep it under three minutes.

Those first cold December nights after I walked out of Dawson's seemed to go on and on. But when I looked at the calendar it hadn't even been a week. I was still trying to keep from thinking about my time in Saint Augustine with Corinne. That was all just locked up somewhere inside, the only thing I had left in reserve, and I wanted to horde it. I had to concentrate on thinking about other stuff to keep from thinking about Corinne. Sally's grandmother told me on the phone that Chris was getting more active in sanatorium social activities. That's what she called it, social activities. I got a kind of chill when she said it, because it sounded like somebody talking about a mental patient in a sewing circle or old folks playing bingo.

I could only picture Chris these days the way she was when I was in the sanatorium, laying there in bed with the TV on, not quite paying attention to whoever was in the room with her. She just seemed to fade further and further away from the land of the living. Maybe I had resigned myself a long time ago that she was bound to die when we found out about the tuberculosis. That didn't seem likely now with the new drugs they were trying, but, deep down I don't think I had stopped thinking that . I wondered if she had been thinking the same thing, and still was. It wasn't the kind of thing to talk about with her, not while she was still in that place.

I hadn't known anything more about TB when she came down with it than the average person. I was as terrified of it as anyone else, something that just sucked you dry and killed you. Against everything the doctors kept telling me about the new drugs and all, that lifelong fear still was running through the back of my mind. I was always half expecting that phone call or a telegram saying she was gone. I kept being surprised by her mother's cheerful reports about how well she was doing, and wondering if she was whistling past the graveyard.

Driving around, I would think about how it would work out if Chris came home again for good, all cured. The idea was kind of scary. Being by myself had been really bad when Chris and Sally first went away. Then that feeling numbed down, and it just seemed odd to be alone all the time. Then one day, without really noticing, it stopped being odd and started being just the way it was and probably was always going to be. I just worked and sent money to make my wife comfortable and keep my kid going, and that was my life. It dawned on me, driving around those first cold nights after my run-in with Dawson, that the idea of going back to living as a family with Chris and Sally made me nervous, even if I didn't believe it was really going to happen.

Although I was absolutely careful not to let my thoughts stray to Corinne and me in Saint Augustine, I always seemed to end up driving by her lane and looking up at the lighted windows of her house from First Street. I already knew all the places to park down on First Street or up on Oak or Palm, anywhere that I could see the windows. It seemed like I'd been doing this all my life, sitting in the dark trying to get a peek into somebody else's life. I'd thought that any chance of anything between Corinne and me was gone when she started taking the taxi home from work every night and had never been more wrong about anything in my life. Then after our day in St. Augustine, I'd begun to relax and think everything was going to be just fine. Which made the second time I'd never been more wrong in my life. Being wrong that badly, twice, in two different directions, just had my head completely befuddled.

By walking out on Dawson, I had cut off any chance of spending time with Corinne at work. I had to do it, to protect her job. But I'd never had a chance to explain that to her. Did she even know why I had walked out like that? All I could do was hope that she might call me again so I could explain, but I couldn't sit at home all day and all night hoping that she'd call. It would drive me stark staring crazy. I had a crazy flash of an idea about writing a note to Corinne, but Mrs. Valland always got the mail as I well knew. Would she open her daughter's mail? Even if she didn't do that she would know something was going on, just by Corinne getting mail from me. I was pretty sure Corinne hadn't told her mother about St. Augustine. Not something to tell your mother. She probably hadn't told about the argument with Dawson either. She couldn't risk Bull Valland finding out and stomping in there to see why Dawson was disrespecting his daughter.

Which left me with the kind of frail hope that Corinne would decide to help Mrs. Valland walk the dog like her kids did once in a while. I thought that maybe she wouldn't run me off if I approached her on the street away from the house. She wouldn't want to make a scene. Maybe we could talk long enough for me to explain to her. So I would just sit there in the car with the lights off and the engine running and the heater on. Once in a while I would see a shadow move in front of a lighted window upstairs, and every night there was the steady blue glow upstairs from a television set. Sometimes I would follow Mrs. Valland when she walked the dog, usually alone but sometimes with the kids, and sometimes I wouldn't. I didn't know what I could say to Mrs. Valland, alone or with Corinne's kids.

Now that I was gone from Dawson's, I didn't even know whether Corinne was home or at work when Mrs. Valland walked the dog. So I began to hang around near Dawson's around closing time, someplace where I could watch who came out. The second time I was there I saw Corinne right away, standing outside the take-out door. She was wearing her leather bomber jacket over her waitress uniform. Seeing that jacket was like getting hit hard in the solar plexus. I couldn't not think about us in St.

Augustine then. I had a hard time breathing, just watching her from down the street.

The cab that showed up was Number Eight. Sometimes it seemed to me like the Beaches Cab Company didn't have any other cabs. Shipwreck was still on nights, because even from that distance I could see him bounce out to go around and open the door for her, like he did for all women. I followed them at a distance. He turned right up her lane, bold as brass. Of course he did, he was a taxi driver, just like Bull Valland ordered. I pulled over to the First Street curb and waited while he dropped her off, went up to the waterfront and turned around, and headed back toward Jacksonville Beach. Some trick of the still cold air that night, I heard Corinne's voice for a minute before her front door shut. The only word I heard plain was "Mama." Life was going on for everybody but me.

Chapter Twenty-Nine

By the time I made three numbers runs without any trouble I began to relax a little. There never seemed to be anybody hanging around any of the pickup points who shouldn't be there. None of the pickups were worried at all. With my commissions already received, I had my regular bills for the month covered, and Christmas too. The salary Ronnie paid me for Sundays and the two midweek graveyards was just gravy.

I had plenty of free time again, too much. Even though I had plenty of reason not to call myself to Billy's attention now, or the Jax Beach cops either, I would cruise by Dawson's at closing time, then sit somewhere close to Corinne's house for a little while each night. I was smoking more than I had in years and my throat had a raw feel to it from all the cigarettes. The only thing that would get me headed back to my apartment was my thirst for a slug of bourbon. I didn't dare start drinking behind the wheel, not now I was running numbers again.

Maybe Corinne was mad at me for the way I walked out and left her to face Dawson alone. It was the only thing I could think to do at the time that would save her job. Maybe she didn't understand that was why I did it. Maybe she thought I was afraid of Dawson, and had run out on her. That would kill me if she thought that.

Maybe she knew about what happens when two people who work at the same place get caught doing something like that, but probably not. She would just be amazed they thought that what we did was any of their business. I wasn't amazed, but I didn't think it was any of their business either. I was still angry as hell at Dawson for his self-righteous attitude.

With my money worries eased up I still was thinking about Christmas presents for the family. Suddenly it just came to me that I ought to buy Corinne a present. I could buy her something really nice. Giving it to her would be a way to open a conversation with her without talking about Dawson, or about St. Augustine.

I couldn't bear to start in to talk about St. Augustine and have her say something to ruin it. I couldn't believe she would do that, but she might. Maybe I was making what had happened out to be a lot more than it was. Maybe it hadn't been a big thing for her, but it was a big thing for me, maybe one of the biggest things in my life. The biggest thing for me that I could remember. I guess that sounds sappy, but that's how it felt to me.

Christmas Eve was going to fall on a Thursday that year, so I would be working. Ronnie kept the truck stop open through all the holidays, because there was always business out on the four-lane. People who had to work would drive to the diner for a meal from as far away as St. Augustine and those little jerkwater farm towns like Spuds and Hastings. They'd drive from Green Cove Springs across that long rickety old bridge over the St. Johns River. Farmers and ranch hands and bridge tenders would be there, along with the long-haul truckers. It seemed like everybody who had to work when no one else did eventually found Below the Border: emergency room doctors and nurses on their way to work, the highway patrol and sheriff's office boys, ambulance drivers. The big trucks were always rolling somewhere, trying to turn a buck, and Ronnie had a contract with Greyhound, too.

Ronnie liked staying open 24 hours a day for people on the road with money to spend and nowhere else to spend it. I arranged with Chris' folks that I would drive over to Lake City Monday after my Sunday shift at

Ronnie's, and stay through Tuesday. We'd have an early Christmas for Sally and her mother. I figured I would get back to the Beaches by Wednesday afternoon in time for my midweek shifts, and find time to take Corinne her present.

When I got my Christmas plan all worked out, I could relax a little, maybe the most I had relaxed since that Below the Border breakfast with Corinne. I tried to call Corinne's house once or twice. Bull always answered the phone and I always hung up quick. I thought I wouldn't try that again, but I did. I woke up around noon on Thursday two weeks before Christmas, and the sunlight was coming in from somewhere, reflected on the ceiling in long ribs where the Venetian blinds broke it up. I heard a motorbike go by outside. The sound was sharp the way it is on clear cold days. The room was dim and quiet and I could almost feel the day pushing in from all around. I was still half-asleep.

I watched my thoughts go around and around about running the numbers again and Dawson, and presents to get for Sally, and they fixed on one thing. I was going to call Corinne. I was going to call her right now. I tried to picture what she would be doing. Probably getting ready to go to work, maybe sitting in her slip while her mother combed her hair. She told me once her mother did that every day before work. I tried to imagine her taking a bath, all fresh and damp, and the smell of her talcum powder. She had been carrying that powder in her little paper bag in St. Augustine.

It was almost like I could smell her bathing right there in my room. I got almost dizzy from it. Something clogged my throat and the blood thumped in my ears. I had it bad all right. I dialed the phone and tried to hold that picture of her in my mind. One of her boys answered. I almost hung up, but then said I had to speak to his mother. My mother or grandmother, the young voice said, very formally. I guess they had to deal with asking that all the time. Your mother, I said. My grandmother handles everything about school, he said. This is the restaurant, I said. He said oh wait a minute.

I could feel the caution go away and wondered what he'd been up to at school that had him nervous. I heard him yell Corinne, hey Corinne, the restaurant's on the phone. He didn't bother to cover the speaker. It still seemed odd that her kids called her by her first name.

She came on and said hello, just like that. I forgot whatever I might have been going to say.

"Hello," I said back.

"Who is this?" She sounded instantly suspicious

"Who do you think?"

"I don't know, and if you don't say right now, I'm hanging up," she said in a cold voice. "All right, goodbye."

"Wait!" I said. "It's me. Walter."

"Oh. Hello." That was all she said. The line hummed.

"How you been?" I said.

"Okay, I guess. You all right?"

"I'm okay. I miss going riding, though."

"Huh." She sounded pleased, though. Maybe I just thought she did. "Have you got a job yet?"

"Part-time, out at Below the Border. I'll probably get on full-time after Christmas."

"You shouldn't have done that, what you did in there with Dawson that day. You didn't have to. I would have got him straightened out. I did, after you left."

"I couldn't stay there." Then it all just came boiling out of me. "He would have fired one of us or both. That's just what bosses do. I couldn't let those ex-husbands have a shot at your boys. I could get a job faster. I couldn't stand there and let him try to say things about..." My throat closed right up. "Us," I finally forced out.

"Don't worry, he ain't said a word since. I think you scared him a little. It was a good job for you though, and I know you need the money. Don't we all."

"I'll be all right. I'll be fine." I was grinning now like an idiot. Call me stupid, but by god it sounded like she had actually been worried about me.

"I still wish you wouldn't have had to lose your job," she said. "That ain't fair."

I couldn't believe how good her taking my side made me feel. I tried to explain. "Even if I could have stayed, somebody would have just had to keep on about it. About us I mean. With me gone there's nothing to talk about.'

"Don't bet on it," she said.

"It'll blow over now that I'm gone," I said. "I didn't want to quit, but sometimes you just have to know when it's time."

"Mama says you don't, though," she said.

"Don't what?" Here she went in some direction whole different direction.

"She says you don't know when to quit. She's seen you watching the house. She's seen you when she was out walking the dog. She says you been calling and hanging up, too. It must have been you. Nobody else would be doing that. She says you got to leave us alone."

"Fuck her!" It came out so fast I couldn't stop it.

"Don't you ever say anything like that again as long as you live," she said. The way she said it scared the hell out of me. "Don't you ever use that word again about a member of my family, not ever again. Mama don't like that word, don't you say it about her."

"I'm sorry," I said. "I didn't mean it, I really didn't mean it, Corinne. I mean, this is just the first time I've talked to you since I quit Dawson's. I haven't bothered anybody. What does she mean I have to stop? Stop what?"

"You've got to stop hanging around, and following me

home, and you've got to stop calling. Daddy knows it's you. He's acting crazy, saying stuff like that Mama and me have been sneaking off with you when he went fishing. He's mad all the time. He's just gone crazy." She said it all so calm, so matter-of-fact.

"But, listen, that really is crazy," I said. "This whole thing is crazy. Why can't we go riding like we used to, and just talk? I could drive you home after work. What's the harm in that? I could save you cab fare every night."

"No," she said.

"But, Corinne--"

"No," she said again. "I thought you said you know when to quit."

"I don't *want* to quit," I said. "I just got started."

"No you didn't either. You never got started, not like you mean." Her voice was so cold it didn't even sound like her. "You got to stop now, you hear? You got to stop. Right now. Today."

"But why?"

"You just got to. Daddy says no daughter of his is goin' to make a joke out of him with some married man. He says he'll kill somebody first. He already ain't buying no Coca Colas for the kids as punishment. He says we ain't going to see another Coca Cola in this house until I make you stop, and they love 'em so good."

"He's cut off the kids' Cokes?" I said. "He's crazy."

"You stop saying that."

"You said it first."

"You shut up, Walter. I ain't going to argue with you. You just stop, you hear?"

"Do you want me to stop?"

"You've got to stop. Don't you understand? It doesn't make no difference what I want."

"It does to me."

"You don't make no difference, either," she said. "Just

194

stop. Please stop."

"But I want to see you. I want to talk to you. We got to talk, Corinne, we just got to." I heard the whiny way I sounded, but I couldn't shut up.

She was back inside whatever twisted prison she had come out of that day in St. Augustine, and she was back inside for good. I could tell that, but I just couldn't turn loose. I just couldn't. I tried to keep her talking but she suddenly said she couldn't talk anymore and hung up, just like that. She didn't even say goodbye.

I know I got to the Below the Border that night, but I don't remember any of it except that I must've tried to call her twenty times. She hung up again on me twice. Then Mrs. Valland started being the one who answered the phone and said Corinne had gone to work. She was cold as ice on the phone. I tried to call Corinne at Dawson's, but Mabel sneered at me and said you know Dawson don't allow no personal calls unless it's an emergency, and hung up on me like I was a total stranger.

Somehow I got through the shift at Ronnie's and took a case of beer home with me the next morning and tried to drink it all as fast as I could, and got the sickest I have ever been from drinking somewhere between the fifth and sixth bottle. I just turned my insides out into the toilet, and then sat there backwards on the stool for I don't know how long, half-asleep, so weak and sick I couldn't even get up and go to bed.

I hadn't even told Corinne I was going to give her a Christmas present. I spent the day in bed with an awful hangover, and tried to call her that afternoon. Mrs. Valland answered again and hung up as soon as she heard my voice. After that, the line was busy, so they must have left the phone off the hook. I drove around some that night, and watched Mrs. Valland walk the dog to the post office. She had both Corinne's boys with her. For reinforcements, I guess. I felt awful and didn't know how to make it right. I went home finally and drank some more beer to cure the hangover and went to bed. In spite of all that had happened since August, it was still just the middle of December, and it looked like Christmas was never going to get here.

Chapter Thirty

I did my Christmas shopping Saturday. The weather stayed cleared off and cold most of the day, and then the clouds started rolling back in. Jacksonville catches a lot of wind in its streets the way it's built in a twisty curve of the St. Johns River. The wind was cold as biddy be damn. All the Christmas lights had been up since Thanksgiving and they turned them on as soon as it turned dark and grey.

There were plenty of people downtown. This was before all those big shopping malls. Downtown was where you went to do serious Christmas shopping. I began to get in the spirit of the crowds and the sick feeling about that conversation with Corinne finally went away. It was going to be all right.

The most expensive present that I got for Sally was one of those Madame Alexander dolls that had first hit the market 1957. It was called the Cissy model, and I remember the name exactly because Sally had pestered us for Cissy from the first day she heard about her. Those Madame Alexander dolls were usually out of my price range, but it was Christmas and I had the *bolita* money so I figured what the hell. Imagining the look on Sally's face when she tore open the pretty blue snowflake wrapping paper made me happy. She liked to get a lot of presents, so I got her two or three little things too, none of which sticks in memory.

Chris' folks were buying what they called her "big Santa Claus" that year, meaning a bicycle and stuff like that. They put Santa Claus gifts out by the Christmas tree after they got home from midnight church service on

Christmas Eve and put Sally to bed, just like my mother did when I was a kid. Thinking about my mom, and about how I would miss Christmas morning with my daughter, kind of choked me up there for a little while. But Sally would get to open my presents before I left, so I tried to think of it like she was going to have two Christmases all her own. I figured two would suit her better than one, especially if one came with a Cissy doll and one came with a new bicycle. Thinking of it that way had me smiling again right along with the Christmas shoppers.

I got Chris a pair of teal -blue pajamas that looked like silk and were really pretty to go with a big clear bottle of the bubble bath she used to like. The soap crystals were the same color as the pajamas. I couldn't remember if she even used bubble bath in the sanatorium. But I figured she probably could use it if she wanted to, and it might help her remember some of the good years. Getting it was kind of a gesture to the days we had before the TB. I found a fancy tie for Chris's dad at the Sears, Roebuck men's department and then bought her mother a big gift-wrapped box of Hollingsworth chocolates. Her mother had always been crazy about that candy. Every Christmas, sooner or later, she would always say that it just wasn't Christmas without a big box of Hollingsworth chocolates in the house. I thought that sounded like a commercial that might have got stuck in her head when she was a girl, but I bought her the Hollingsworth anyway. I had bought her a box every Christmas since Chris and I got married. The people at the department store wrapped everything real nice, a lot better than I could have, and looking at them all in the trunk of the Chev I began to feel like Christmas was going to come after all.

I went to a fancy perfume store and got Corinne the biggest bottle of Chanel No. 5 that I could afford. I blew the rest of my *bolita* money on it and it still looked kind of small to me. Jesus, it was expensive, even back then. The saleslady was kind of snooty and said you don't want to mess up a gift like this with cheap department store wrapping paper. She wrapped the perfume for me personally in expensive-looking white tissue paper with green and gold ribbon and a nice bow at the top. She had a fancy looking card for me to sign to go with it. When she was done, all the other presents except the doll package looked a little tacky in comparison. I guess the saleslady's snootiness infected me. I even thought about trying to get the presents all re-wrapped to look as nice as Corinne's, but didn't have any idea how to go about it so I just let it go. If I was going to buy nice things for a woman not my wife, I figured that was the kind of thing I had to learn to live with.

I carried Corinne's present home in a double shopping bag for extra protection. When I left the apartment Monday morning to go over to Lake City, I took her present out of the shopping bags and left it sitting in the center of the kitchen table so it would be the first thing I saw when I got back. Usually that drive to Lake City was one of my favorite things to do, out on the open road with the Chev purring like it was ready to roll clear to California if I took a notion. I should have been happy thinking about being with Sally at Christmas-time. But I started thinking about that last conversation with Corinne again and got down in the dumps again.

The more I thought about it, the more I thought about calling her again to try to get things straightened out between us. I wanted to call her really bad, but I tried to keep from thinking about doing it. When I couldn't keep from thinking about calling her anymore, I tried to keep from actually looking for a roadside phone booth up ahead to do it from. But I wanted at least to let her know that I had her Christmas present. I was afraid she might try to call my apartment and I wouldn't be there.

She might try to call me since our last conversation had been interrupted. If she couldn't get me, she might even think I got scared off and was gone for good. I couldn't bear the thought that she might think I got scared off. She might think I gave up on her if she called my apartment and I wasn't there to answer. My thoughts just kept going around and getting sillier and more desperate-like.

Finally I stopped at that old truck stop near Olustee and got some quarters from the cashier and dialed the long-distance operator from one of the phone booths in front of the long-haul truckers' shower room. When Mrs. Valland heard the long-distance operator on the line she didn't even think about it being me and called Corinne to the phone right away. In the 1950s an unexpected long-distance call meant something serious to people, just like a Western Union telegram in the night did. I knew no one who answered the phone would think of it being me, not calling long-distance. Corinne recognized my voice the minute I spoke to her.

"Where you at?" she said. "You ain't on the Beaches, not calling long-distance. Not unless you got Mabel or somebody to fake it."

I had to smile at that. I would never have thought of that, and Mabel probably wouldn't have done it for me anyway.

"No," I said, "it really is long distance. I'm on my way to see Sally and the family in Lake City. But I'll be back on the Beaches before Christmas."

"So what?"

"I got a present for you, that's so what. Something special for a special person."

"Oh, for God's sake," she said. I thought at first she was going to call me corny. Maybe even she thought she was going to. But I could tell she hadn't been expecting anything like that.

"You didn't have to do that," she said finally.

"I don't have to do anything but die and pay taxes," I said. "I wanted to."

"That's nice of you to say," she said.

I could tell she was pleased and trying to hide it. When was there ever a woman not pleased that a man wanted to give her a special present? It had probably been a long time since any man gave her a real present, at Christmas or any other time.

"I'll bring it by when I get back," I said.

She made a little sound, like a groan. "Daddy's going to take a peace bond out on you for sure. He's already complained to the phone company about you calling, but they said they couldn't do anything about that."

"It's just a Christmas present," I said. "Why can't I at least give you a Christmas present? Don't people give each other Christmas presents in Georgia?"

"But I don't have anything for you!" She sounded like she felt bad about not having a Christmas present for me and my heart just turned over again, just like it did with her in St. Augustine.

"That don't matter," I said. "Giving you a present is present enough for me. I mean it, Corinne. Can't I at least give you a Christmas present?"

"Oh, all right," she said. "I've got to go now, certain people are coming up the stairs."

I felt so much better after that phone call that I listened to Christmas carols on the radio all the way to Lake City. Chris's parents had up a big Christmas tree in the living room. Sally was helping decorate by hanging ornaments as high as she could reach. Chris's old man already had all the tree lights on, including a lot of those multi-colored bubbling lights that looked kind of like glass candles that were a big thing back then.

Him and me finished the rest of the tree off, and he put the angel on top. Then we sat down to look at the tree and have some Canadian Club to celebrate Christmas. I leaned back and stared at the twinkling lights and felt more peaceful and calm than I had in a long time. For once my separate lives here and at the Beaches seemed to both be under control.

Later, I brought in the Christmas presents from the car and put them under the tree while Sally was eating supper. After dessert, Sally had a fit trying to guess what was in hers, and started in on me to open just one tonight, maybe just the big blue one with the snowflakes. I held out for the next day, and we all went to bed early. I slept like a log and woke up hearing Sally downstairs somewhere singing Hark the Herald Angels Sing in her high sweet voice. It felt almost like home, real home, listening to her under Chris' mom's handmade quilts. I lay there a long time and thought about Ohio Christmases when I was a kid, and the first Christmas after Sally was born and how the tree lights reflected in her big round baby eyes, the times in my life when I had been completely happy. But even then Corinne always was in the back of my mind.

Tuesday night they let Christine out of the sanatorium for a couple of hours for dinner. Her folks were real excited and had some family friends over. Her mom even baked a cake with the candles for Chris's last birthday, though her birthday had been six months ago. It turned into a real party. Chris and I hardly had time to speak a word to just each other.

Seeing Chris away from the hospital room was a real shocker. She had looked pale and quiet in the sanatorium, but in among other people with faces pink from all the holiday cheer they were taking in, she looked more like those World War Two photographs of prisoners of war.

She looked thin and shrunken up and confused by all the talking and laughing. She asked Sally to blow out the birthday candles for her. After we got that part over, and before any of the rest of us finished eating dinner, Chris got up and went into the living room and turned on the television and just sat there in the dark staring at the screen like she was back in the sanatorium.

After dinner, we all moved into the living room and started in on her old man's liquor. Nobody smoked indoors out of respect to Chris's lungs, and the ones that just had to have their after-dinner nicotine kept going out on the back porch and coming back in a steady stream. I went out there too, and they all told me how good Christine looked, really healthy.

I guess they couldn't say anything else on Christmas. Everybody talked at her and around her but she just kept staring at the TV with the sound turned off and didn't say much of anything at all.

I asked her let's go for a walk together outside. She said it's too cold, and I can't, almost in the same breath, without even looking at me. I stood there over her until I finished my CC, and she didn't look up the whole time. She just seemed vaguely bothered because I wouldn't go away. I just kept looking at her and feeling the walls closing in. I had a sudden terrible hope that she never would come home again, ever, if this was all there was left of her. I was ashamed of myself for thinking it, and my ears got hot from all the liquor.

The nurse took her back to the sanatorium in a taxi, and everybody else immediately loosened up and stayed around and got pretty drunk before the evening was over. When the last visitors left it was almost Sally's bedtime, but we let her stay up to open my presents and for her grandparents to open the ones I got them. They got me to open one of mine, but I wanted to take the rest back with me to open after I got off work, so I could make Christmas last.

The one I opened was a tie from Sally, crisp blue and green regimental stripes with a phony crest on it. Her grandfather winked at me, held up his tie that I got him, and said it looked like we both were going to be better dressed in the new year. Sally said she didn't want her grandpa to have more ties than her dad is why she gave me a tie, because everybody knew I always bought grandpa a tie. Everybody got a good laugh out of that. Sally of course had to rip into the snowflake package first, and she let out quite a squeal when she saw the doll.

"Cissy! I love Cissy, Dad!"

"I kind of knew that," I said. I was grinning so hard my jaws hurt.

Sally cuddled the doll to her and began to coo at it in baby talk. Her grandparents were beaming at me like I was a pretty smart guy after all. Then Sally had to parade Cissy around the entire house to show her her new home, and then it was her bedtime. I went up to tuck her in, and she had the doll snuggled in the curve of her arm just like a miniature of her mother with her that first Christmas. I had to swallow a lump as big as my fist to say goodnight in a normal tone of voice.

"Don't worry, Daddy," Sally said in her little-girl sleepy voice. "I really love Cissy, but I love you best of all. And Mommy best of all too," she added as her eyes drifted shut. "And grandma and grandpa best of all three." Her grandmother politely pretended I didn't have tears running down my face as we went downstairs together.

Chris was going to come back on Christmas Day for dinner and to see Sally's new bicycle and stuff. I liked to think of Chris there with her family instead of in that sanatorium. I was over wishing she would never come home. Sure she would. She would get completely well one of these days and we could start all over as a family. I thought maybe she would relax more without me around. I hoped so anyway. We'd work on getting used to each other again, all in due time. It'd be okay.

Chris's mother carried on in a big way about the Hollingsworth chocolates I got her, the way she always did. We all had to have some of the candy of course. I got the caramel, which is my favorite, but it tasted funny after all the Canadian Club. Chris's mom got up early Wednesday to fix me breakfast and a pot of black coffee for my hangover before I got on the road. I left before Sally was awake.

The weather was cold and grey and looked almost like it might really snow, Florida or not. The highway was quiet and empty that early, and once I was really out on the road and headed back to the Beaches, I started getting so excited about Corinne's present that I could hardly stand it. I had made it through the rough part of Christmas, having to see Chris looking like that and having to leave Sally again. Now I could put that behind me, and now came the part about giving Corinne her Chanel No. 5. I bet her cheapskate ex-husbands never gave her anything like that.

I was pretty sure she would like it but I had it all arranged so she could take it back and exchange it after Christmas if she didn't. I hoped she would like it, though. The saleslady had said that getting that kind of perfume from a gentleman friend--that's how she put it, a gentleman friend--was something very special to a woman, because it was the very best. I hoped it hadn't been just a sales pitch. I couldn't wait to see Corinne's face when I gave it to her. I had never given her anything but rides home and driving lessons. Our day in St. Augustine, she had given me something I would remember always, that no one could ever take away from me no matter what ended up happening. I wanted to see her face when she opened her Christmas present so bad that it almost hurt.

Chapter Thirty-One

When I hit the Beaches the streets were almost totally deserted, and a big northeast wind was blowing again. Dead palm fronds jumped and flew across Beach Boulevard. Seagulls either hung on the wind like Christmas-tree ornaments or huddled out of the wind on flat roofs along the boardwalk. A lot of restaurants already were closed for Christmas, so I went on home and made myself a Denver omelet and laid down to rest for a while.

It was full dark when I got up and showered and shaved and put on my next best suit or my worst one, depending on which way you counted. I would have worn my other one but I didn't want it to get kitchen smells in it out at the Below the Border when I changed into whites later. The Mermaid Lounge had the only lighted open sign that I saw near the boardwalk, so I stopped in for a shot. The place had more people in it than I expected, a lot of sailors who hadn't been able to go home for Christmas and a few hard-drinking locals who thought the Mermaid was home. Jerry was behind the bar, and asked me if I was on my way to church. I said no why, and he said he had never seen me in a suit before.

"Did somebody die? No, I guess that's Easter," he said. That Jerry always was a card.

"You don't have to have a special reason to get dressed up on Christmas Eve," I said.

"If you ain't going to midnight services and you ain't going to a funeral, you must be going sparking, don't hand me that double talk," he said.

"Just give me a bourbon." I had had enough Canadian whisky for a while.

"I thought you were on beer, steady."

"It's Christmas Eve," I said.

"Think of all the crimes committed in the name of Christianity," Jerry said. He just never let up. He slid a shot across the bar and I knocked it back neat. His bar whiskey was Old Crow, which was some of the stoutest bourbon around in those days, if not the fanciest. The heat spread up from my belly clear to my eyeballs and made them water. The last vestiges of my hangover headache went away. I slid the glass back.

"That broke the chill. Hit me again."

"Dutch courage," Jerry said, and filled the glass. "You're going sparking, without a doubt. I hear you're working for Ronnie again."

"I ain't working for Dawson anyway."

"You look like the change did you good. You put on any more weight and you'll have to have that suit let out some."

"I've been eating pretty heavy, all right." I hadn't thought about it until he said it, but now I noticed the crotch of my pants did feel a little snug, and the armpits of the coat too. I shifted around to try to loosen it up.

"You must have a hot date, the way you can't sit still," Jerry said.

"Now don't you start that crap," I said. "I don't expect that crap from my friends."

"I don't mean nothin' by it, Walter, you know that. It's just that you was playing with yourself there, right on the barstool."

"The crotch is a little tight, that's all. I guess I am gaining a little weight like you say."

"Hell, Walter, you ain't supposed to gain weight from eating that kind of dish, even if it is the sweetest there is." He let out a big haw-haw and walked away from me before I could get mad. I was going to have to quit letting all that crap bother me. The more I let it get my goat, the more they'd do it, even my friends. Maybe especially my friends. I wished they'd stop, though.

I finished the second shot of Old Crow slow and let the liquor work me over a little, smoothing down my nerves. I was in quite a state, all right. A little while later, Jerry came back by.

"Another?"

"No thanks."

"C'mon, on the house. To make up for that last crack." He paused, then went haw-haw again, real hard. "Jesus Christ, there I go again. It's these sailors they're moving into Mayport. They're a bad influence on me. Guess I didn't have that far to fall, though, huh?" He went haw-haw again, to show he hadn't meant anything.

"Can I take a raincheck? I got a package to drop off. I might need a drink after that."

He thought I meant a numbers run. "Hell, I didn't know the *bolita* ran on Christmas. I thought all those Cubans was Catholic, let alone the Eyetalians." Well, let him think what he wanted.

"I got hospital bills to pay, among other things," I said.

"Yeah, I know. Listen, just walk careful, okay? I think Billy is keeping an eye on you, almost like it's personal. It wouldn't do for you to get caught doing that kind of work."

"Thanks for the word," I said. "I'll be careful."

"Think nothin' of it. Come on back by for that shot on the house. Hell, it's Christmas, come on back for two."

I said I would and went out into the northeaster. My mind was a blank. I kept trying to think of things I could say to her. I wondered if Bull would be home. Probably, since it was Christmas Eve.

Dawson's was closed and dark when I went by, so Dawson had missed putting together a big Christmas party to make up some of his losses. It served him right, the self-righteous prick.

All the lights in Corinne's house seemed to be on when I turned up her lane. My hands were cold by then, and not just from the weather. I couldn't swallow, my throat was so dry. The Old Crow made my face hot and heavy, and I felt damp under my clothes. I drove up to the dead-end at ocean front, backed it around and parked in front of her house, half out in the lane. There was a record-player going somewhere in the house. It was Gene Autry singing an old Christmas favorite called Old-Fashioned Tree You couldn't mistake that voice: "Star light, shinin' on the snow--wishin' star of Christmas time..." The record sounded old and scratchy. The Singing Cowboy had pretty much retired from singing by then and started building his business empire.

I took Corinne's present off the front seat and walked up to the door. For a minute, I couldn't hear Gene Autry anymore, just my own blood thumping in my ears. I pushed the door bell and it seemed to ring somewhere far off, like down a tunnel. I heard a rocking chair stop rocking upstairs. I heard somebody walk across to the window to look out. I was under the overhang but they could see the Chev all right. Then I heard somebody walking downstairs too, somebody whistling Jingle Bells loud against the Gene Autry record.

The door swung open and he stopped in mid-whistle and I stopped breathing. It was Bull Valland. Way off I could hear footsteps coming down from upstairs and hoped it was Corinne. Bull and me just kept staring at each other. The only glimpse I ever had of that face looking relaxed and happy was in that split second as he swung the door open. Now that Indian look was back again. Behind the stare it seemed like he was thinking that he couldn't believe his own eyes, that I would dare to be on his doorstep.

We stood there and the footsteps from upstairs came through the living room now, and it was Mrs. Valland, not Corinne. Her face looked like it had been carved out of some old pale wood or ivory. Nothing as mean as Bull, something a lot more fragile and fine, but just as angry. I tried to speak, couldn't, tried again and got it out.

"I brought Corinne a Christmas present," I said. "May I see her, please?" It didn't sound like me talking. It sounded like that comedian Don Knotts on the Steve Allen TV show. Worse. It sounded like Chip and Dale, those cartoon chipmunks. It sounded awful.

"That's very nice," Mrs. Valland said, like she was talking to me from the other side of the moon. "Just give it to me, Walter, and I will see that she gets it."

"I would prefer to give it to her, please." I sounded like an idiot.

"I am sorry," she said as formally as a queen, "Corinne is not at home." Polite to the bitter end. But she had to be lying. It was Christmas Eve for Christ's sake. I had thought of everything that might happen but her not being here. I couldn't think what to say next.

"But I need to see her," I said. Squeaked, rather. "It's Christmas Eve."

Bull finally spoke. "Why, you son-of-a-bitch, I don't believe it," he said.

"Bull," Mrs. Valland said. I had never heard her call him that. She sounded talking to an unruly dog.

"Shut up," he said to her. When he looked back at me, I forgot everything except to be scared. The way he looked at me, my God, I can wake up sweating even now just to dream about that look. "You son-of-a-bitch," he said. "You sorry little son-of-a-bitch. I never I really thought you'd have the nerve to come right up to this door again."

He sounded choked up with rage, But in an odd way he sounded happy at the same time, a kind of happy that will freeze my bowels every time I think of it until the day I die.

Then he hit me. He just drew back and hit me square in the chest. It felt like getting hit by a car. Then it felt like a car had run into me from behind almost in the same instant. That was my car when I bounced off it and went down on the pavement. Shattuck had hit me in the face twice and knocked me down and almost unconscious. I had been hit hard before Shattuck, too. But never anything like Bull hit me.

I was sitting on the ground flat on my ass and my crotch was cold as ice where my pants had split open, and my head felt so hollow I thought he'd knocked my brains out even though he hadn't hit me in the face. I couldn't breathe. My lungs felt like crumpled up wet cardboard boxes. I couldn't move, either. I couldn't even raise my head off my shoulder, so that the two of them seemed like sidewise black cutouts standing in the door, with the light pouring out around them and Gene Autry still singing.

But I wasn't even close to unconscious. There was no going away like there had been when Shattuck hit me. I was all hunched up around my caved-in lungs and wondering if my heart had stopped. Bull was stepping toward me like a giant, with the light from the house glowing on his shoulders and his face in darkness. He was drawing back his foot. It seemed like he drew it back a long, long way - like his heel was going to hit the overhang - and his eyes glittered at me in the shadows like coal on fire.

He was going to drop - kick me right over the top of my own car and out into the cold wind, spinning like a football. I knew that I was going to die, right there. Flat on my ass and trying to scream no please, I was going to get squashed in like a cockroach.

Somewhere way up above my head I heard an awful,

meat-cleaver sound. Suddenly Bull's raised leg just dropped. The giant grunted and collapsed all in a heap, boneless. He crashed into the car beside me. I felt the Chev wobble hard on its springs. I stared at the empty door where he had stood and didn't understand.

The Gene Autry record had caught in a groove and kept going "trimmed with tinsel, trimmed with tinsel", over and over. I just sat there trying to draw some air into my lungs.

Then a face came into focus down close to mine. It was Mrs. Valland. "You get up," she said. Her voice was like an icepick in a block of ice. "You get up now and you go away from here before he wakes up and kills you, you heah?"

I sucked in air and tried to speak. I bubbled instead. Hot flashes kept shooting across my eyes.

"You get up," Mrs. Valland said again in that same icy voice. "You get up and you go die somewhere else."

Her face went away, and I heard her from what seemed a long distance off, softer now, like a mother talking to a sick child, saying, "Bull, Bull, wake up now, Bull, I didn't hit you that hard. You got a thick skull anyway."

I heard a kind of sick groan and he shifted against me, but not much. I finally got some air in my lungs. They ached like fire. I rolled away from him and got hold of the car-door handle and pulled myself up little by little. Then I leaned on the roof and tried not to fall back down, with my feet spread as wide as I could.

"Close your legs, for God's sake," came that soft cold voice. "Your pants are split wide open, show a little decency, can't you?"

She was crouched above Bull, cupping his face in her hands, trying to get him to stir. His head was propped against the car now and he was on his back. He was breathing heavy, almost snoring. A bulging man's sock swung heavily from Mrs. Valland's right hand. It thudded against the car with a little bong, like a bell. It was stuffed with something heavy.

"Is he dead?" I said.

"You get out of here," she said. "Go on, leave."

"Where's Corinne, Mrs. Valland?"

"That's none of your God-damned business!" The profanity, coming in her soft drawl, shocked me. I smelled something sweet and heavy in the air all around us, so thick it made my head swim.

"Where's Corinne's Christmas present?" I said.

"It broke all over the pavement," Mrs. Valland said. "It broke when you fell down and dropped it. Now go on, get out of here."

"That was forty dollars' worth of perfume," I said. I was finally getting some breath back, and getting mad over the top of my fear. "It was a Christmas present for Corinne. Who does he think he is to do that to me? To break her Christmas present?"

"You shut up right now," she said. "You say another word and I'll call Ben. He's there upstairs now with his .22 rifle , and he's crazy mad to get a shot at you to impress his granddaddy. Ben never makes nothing but head shots on squirrels, so you don't want him to shoot you, even with a .22. Neither do I. He won't come unless I call him, but I'll call him unless you leave right now. I'll count to three."

"But -"

"I'll count to three. I mean it now."

"I just wanted to give her a Christmas present, for Christ's sake!"

"For your sake, you mean. Corinne ain't here, and your Christmas present is broke. I'm counting: One."

"Where else would she be on Christmas Eve?"

"That ain't your concern. Two."

I stumbled around the car and got in. I couldn't get the

thick smell of the perfume out of my nose. I almost reached for the pistol under the seat, but Bull was still out cold. Who was I going to shoot, a crazy old woman with a heavy sock for a sap, or a kid with a .22 rifle?

I sat there trying to get my mind clear. Mrs. Valland crouched in the right hand window like a vicious little old monkey. "I don't hear your car starting," she said. "You get out of here now before I count three."

There wasn't anything else to do. I started the engine and got out of there.

Chapter Thirty-Two

I was shaking so bad I could hardly hold the car on the road, but I made it back to the Mermaid and parked in a loading zone by the front door. Then I got inside on a bar stool, still having trouble with my breathing. Jerry came over with a bourbon already poured and did a double-take.

"Good God, what happened to you?"

I drained the drink off and choked when it bit into me. I couldn't talk, not yet. I just shook my head and pointed at the glass. He filled it up. I put that back in one long pull, and got to shuddering so bad I almost tipped off the bar stool. I laid my head down on my arms and waited for the room to stop spinning.

"You want me to call an am'blance?" Jerry said.

"No."

"Trouble from a customer? Want me to call Ronnie ?" He thought some sore loser had roughed me up. I pushed myself off the bar and tried to focus on him but he kept blurring.

"Pershonal," I said. It was the first time since I started drinking at age sixteen that I ever slurred an S.

"Oh, shit," Jerry said. "Not Shattuck again."

"Who's calling me?" said a voice from in back of me. "Is that Walter up there with you now, Jerry? Walter the sex fiend, I mean?"

"Who let you in here?" Jerry threw back at him. "When did you crawl in?"

"While you were waterin' them sailors' drinks, you cheapster," Shattuck said. It was him, all right. Oh God no, not him too, not now, kept going over and over in my mind. I heard a chair scrape back under the jukebox noise.

Oh God oh God here he came, up to the bar.

"You go back over there and mind your own business," Jerry told him, but he said it weak. A lot of them around the Beaches were more than half-afraid of Shattuck and his bunch.

"Watcha doin' in your fancy suit, Walter?" Shattuck said. "Crying in your liquor? Got stood up again, huh? The new man's makin' all the time that's gonna get made, that it? I don't blame you boy, it's your gal, I'll give you that, but it's my cab that they keep getting the back seat sticky, doin' you know what. It gets me jealous too, them doin' it in my cab, you better believe it" He leaned closer. "Hell, Walter, you smell like a French whorehouse."

"You get out of here," Jerry said to him. "You got no call to come in here saying stuff like that about Walter's girlfriend. Drink up and get out."

"You gonna make me?"

"What are you talking about, doing it in your cab?" I said.

"Shattuck's just drunk and being mean, Walter," Jerry said. "He's just mad because they put him back on days and cut his hours back and he ain't making any money."

"I ain't making any of what Shipwreck is making, that's for sure, and not just money either," Shattuck said. "Ol' Shipwreck is takin' it in trade, and right in my cab damn the luck. I always thought eight was my lucky number, too. I guess you got her tuned up during the summer all right, Walter, but it's Shipwreck who takes her for a spin 'most every night now."

"You are a filthy rotten son-of-a-bitch," I said. It hurt to get all that out with my lungs still burning, but I did, and he heard every word, too. So did everybody else in the place. Somebody had pulled the plug on the jukebox. I hadn't even noticed until I heard how loud my voice sounded.

"Now don't you start again with me, Walter," Shattuck said. His voice turned mean. "Don't you go getting on your high horse with me about some two-bit whore who dishes it out for anybody who'll ride her home free. And I do mean ride. It woulda been me getting some of that if I hadn't got switched to days. That pisses me off, sure, but don't you go taking on airs about that cunt, or me and Lenny will do you worse than we did the last time."

I swung around. Shattuck was up close to me and Lennie was right behind him, grinning that idiot grin in the dim light from the bar. I tried to smash my fist into Shattuck's lying teeth and he ducked and I missed. The bar stool swiveled around and I fell off and hit the floor hard on my left side. Everything got quiet. The bar stool kept squeaking, turning around and around. There wasn't another sound, now. Both of them just stood there grinning at me while I got up.

"You all saw it," Shattuck said real loud. "I ain't going to do nothing now but defend myself."

"Not in my bar," Jerry said, just as loud. "By god not in here you don't, or I'll have you in jail so long you'll be on social security when you get out. You too, Lennie. I mean it!"

"All right," Shattuck said. He was looking at me with almost exactly the same expression on anticipation that Bull had before his wife sapped him with the loaded sock. Then he looked at Lennie and grinned. "Let's take Walter the sex fiend outside and teach him a Christmastime lesson, Lennie."

"Not two on one," Jerry said. "I'm calling Billy."

Lennie leaned across the bar. "Hand me the phone, Jerry."

"Huh?"

"Hand me the God-damned phone."

It looked like Jerry was going to refuse. But in the end,

he didn't. Lennie gave the phone a big yank and snatched its cord out of the wall. Then he tossed the phone on the floor. It made an awful jangle in the dead quiet. Lennie looked at me.

"Let's go outside, you little shit. We've got some settling up to do for that busted beer bottle."

I looked at Jerry. He looked away. People were already shuffling their feet, ready to run outside behind us to watch the fun. All for a Roman holiday as Mrs. Valland would have said. There wasn't any Mrs. Valland the gun moll standing behind them with a heavy sock. Nobody else was going to help me either.

"I've got a better idea," Shattuck said. He was snuffling that huh-huh-huh laugh of his. "Let's take him over to Shipwreck's and do him right in front of her, because she's over there right now. That'll teach 'em both a lesson. Maybe we should thump on ol' Shipwreck too, for humping her in my cab."

While he was still talking, I turned and ran for the door as hard as I could. Lennie let out a yell and came after me quick, but I got through the swinging doors first. The backswing slowed him down enough for me to get to my car before they caught up with me. All the people in the bar came out in a solid push behind them. Run, Walter, run you little shit, I heard a woman yell, and they all laughed.

I would have got away if I hadn't locked the car door when I went in. It was that close. I had my door half open when Shattuck grabbed me. I hung onto the door frame and tried to shake him off. Lennie was dancing around behind him, trying to get in a punch. I just kept trying to pull loose.

All I could think about was that I couldn't believe she was at Shipwreck's apartment right here on the Beaches, not Shipwreck, he was afraid of his own shadow, let alone somebody like Bull Valland. But I had to get over there to see, I just had to. Shattuck half-pulled my suit coat off and it threw him off-balance. I got one arm loose from the sleeve and pushed him, and he went over backward. The coat came loose in his hands. I heard it rip like my pants had. It didn't matter.

I got in the seat and almost got the keys in the ignition before Lennie grabbed me and tried to haul me out. I hung onto the steering wheel for dear life. He clubbed my fingers loose and dragged me out. I grabbed the doorframe again on the way out and we went down on the pavement. I was kneeling into the car and Lennie was half on top of me when Shattuck pushed him aside and hit me, hard, in the kidneys. My whole lower body seemed to go numb. Shattuck tried to hoist me out of the car. He was trying to pull with one hand and punch with the other, so none of the punches landed real solid. I could hear people yelling in the street and Lennie cussing somewhere behind Shattuck, trying to get back at me. Big waves of black seemed to be rolling over my head.

Then I had my hand under the seat and the .45 in my hand, heavy and solid. I just relaxed and let Shattuck pull us both out onto the pavement. I came out all balled up like a baby. Shattuck hunched over me on his knees to try to straighten me out and flop me around so he could hit me in the face. Lenny kicked me somewhere down along my leg, but my legs were already numb and it didn't seem to hurt. I had the gun up now, the front sight wedged under Shattuck's belt, and I knew I was into him good and I yanked the trigger.

The gun jumped and he jumped, and his fist bounced off my shoulder. He was kneeling back spraddle-legged. The fist he'd tried to hit me with was holding him up. His other hand was trying to hold a thick flow leaking out between his fingers, shining black in the streetlights. He was scared of me now, all right. Scared of me at last.

"You son-of-a-bitch," Lennie said. He was backing away into the street. "You son-of-a-bitch, you shot him!"

I took hold of the gun with both hands and sighted into Lennie's middle. I knew it was all over now, all over for good. The gun made a flash like lightning and a big boom that echoed back from the storefronts and was lost on the wind. I hadn't even heard the first shot.

Lennie went down, *kerplunk*. Not spinning around and waving his arms like they do in the movies. Just down, like all his strings were cut at once and didn't make a sound.

Shattuck was staring at me, his mouth open and twitching like one of those worthless salt-water catfish they toss up on the beach for the seagulls to peck the eyes out of. I suddenly remembered what he had said to me that night at Bennett's Motel.

"How do *you* like it now, you prissy little shit?" I said.

His eyes got wider than I could believe. His mouth twisted open and he tried to say something. Whatever it was got lost in the big boom of the gun, loud enough to crack your eardrums, a heavy jump in my hands and the muzzle flash blinding me. Shattuck went over backwards, flat, his legs twisted up under him with his feet splayed out. His arms flopped out all loose and rubbery. I could see dark blood on the pavement behind him. It must have sprayed out ten feet when the second one went through.

I got up like an old, old man. The salt wind came roaring down the street from the beach and carried off the smell of gunpowder. All I could smell then was Chanel No. 5 on my ripped clothes, mixed with the ocean smell.

Somebody started toward me. It was Jerry. Nobody else had moved or looked like they were going to. My ears were ringing from the shots.

"Jesus, Walter," Jerry said. "Look what you've done.

Oh Jesus. And on Christmas Eve, too."

I was way away somewhere, past everything. "That's two less piles of shit in this world," I said. My voice sounded big as the wind, and I had never felt stronger or more in charge of things in my life. I picked my keys off the floorboard and got back in the car and started it and drove out of there before any of them could think of anything else to say.

Chapter Thirty-Three

*E*verybody mostly knew where everybody else lived on the Beaches. I knew Shipwreck lived in one of those two-story apartment buildings built around a central court that were pretty new on the Beaches then. All I needed to see was the Number Eight cab parked in front of one of them to nail it down.

It was raining again, coming in sheets sideways, when I parked behind the cab. When I got out of the car the hard cold rain drenched the front of my dress shirt and slashed my eyes and made it hard to see. Then the wind eased up for a minute, and I heard the thin wail of an ambulance siren off in the direction of downtown. I started up the walk. I still had the gun in my hand. I hadn't turned it loose even to drive. I shoved it down into my front pants pocket. It was almost too big to fit, but those old pleated suit pants had deep front pockets back then.

I stopped partway up the walk when a man and a woman stepped into view under the arch from the inner courtyard. They stood looking out at the rain and shook out long winter coats. The man was a Navy officer in full-dress blues, white flying saucer cap and all. He was shrugging into one of those heavy officer's bridge coats and the wind was snatching at the tails, making it awkward. He finally got into it and took off his white saucer cap to wipe a handkerchief across his bald dome, and it was Shipwreck. Shipwreck, dressed like Humphrey Bogart playing Captain Queeg,

The woman with him had her hair piled up under a stylish little pillbox hat with a silly scrap of dark veil that came halfway down her forehead, but it was Corinne all right. She was wearing a beautiful dark blue wool dress and now Shipwreck was helping her into a black overcoat with a nice fur collar. The gun butt still stuck out of my pocket a little. I put my hands in my pockets to hide it and walked up to them.

When I came into the light from the archway, Shipwreck acted like he'd seen a ghost the way he snatched his hands away from her shoulders and stepped back so fast. I didn't care about him and his fancy uniform. I had my eyes on Corinne. She looked beautiful enough to break your heart.

"Hello, Walter," she said. "Come in out of the rain. What'd you do, go and spill a ketchup bottle on your white shirt out there at the truck stop?"

"That's not ketchup," Shipwreck said. He was watching me real careful. I walked under the archway out of the rain.

"I thought you got drummed out of the Navy," I said to him for something to say.

He straightened right up. 'Nossir. I have a right to wear this uniform. I am honorably retired on disability."

"I never thought of dipsomania as a disability," I said.

He blinked and licked his lips like they were dry.

"Walter, what a mean thing to say!" Corrine said. "You should apologize to Arthur right this minute."

Here she went again, just like she did when we first went riding, like nothing at all was different. Taking me in hand to re-raise me according to Georgia standards of politeness, like she had about littering the rich people's lawns. It put a hell of a lump in my throat.

"Who's Arthur?" I said.

"That's my name," Shipwreck said. "My real name." He said it like some schoolyard kid daring a bully to make something of it. He was keeping a nervous eye on my hands because he thought I was the bully now. He was plenty scared, but I could see that he didn't want to show it wearing that uniform. It didn't make me feel very good.

"I never knew your name," I told him. "Corinne's right. I apologize for that crack. Nobody with all those ribbons on his chest deserves a crack like that."

"That's better," Corinne said. "Saying something mean just isn't like you, Walter."

"A lot of things aren't like me tonight, Corinne."

I felt stupid standing there in front of her all soaking wet, with my pants split open and rain dripping off my face, when she was dressed so nice and Shipwreck looked like he belonged on Nimitz's staff. I wasn't sure now why I had even come over here.

"Shattuck again?" Shipwreck said. He kept darting his eyes from the smear of blood on my shirt to the heavy sag of my pocket like he was trying to semaphore some question that he was afraid to come right out and ask. He looked like he could really use a drink, too, fancy uniform or no fancy uniform.

"Yeah, Shattuck," I said. "Saying things about you-know-who. Nasty things."

"Dammit – excuse me, Corinne – he's got to stop doing that crap."

"He has stopped," I said. "He'll never do it again. Nor Lennie Cross either."

"Jesus, Walter! Both of them?"

I just nodded.

Shipwreck took his time squaring up his white Navy hat on his head just so. He took a deep breath and squared his shoulders up in that Navy bridge coat. It looked too official for somebody like Shipwreck to be wearing it. Hell, he looked too official to even be Shipwreck. He was plenty scared, but stiffening up his spine to face it head-on.

"Now, Walter," he said. "You gonna do what you have to do. I see that. But I have something to say to you and I want you to listen to me. All right?"

"What could you have to say to me?" I was too busy looking at Corinne again to pay him much attention.

"I want you to know that anything Shattuck may have said to you about you-know-who is absolute crap."

"I always knew that," I said. "But he said some other stuff too, tonight. Which is why I came here."

"That's what I figured." He took a deep breath. "Now Walter, you do what you think you have to do. Just as long as I'm sure that you know that Shattuck is a lying prick – excuse me, Corinne – about every single thing he ever said about you-know-who. Tonight, or any other night, and with anybody – especially me."

"Arthur, mind your language, it's Christmas!" Corinne said.

Here she went trying to re-raise Shipwreck, and him a cashiered sailor and a drunk on top of that. I guess I could have felt jealous. But that was just Corinne, alone in her own private world, and she would be like that till hell froze over. Maybe even after. Goddamn me for a Dutchman if Shipwreck didn't half-bow to her and touch the bill of his hat, like a salute.

"Excuse my language, Corinne," he said. "I know it's Christmas Eve and we're on the way to church. But that's all Shattuck is, nothing put a lying prick and that's all he's ever been. You know that don't you, Walter?"

"What did you say? You're on the way to church?"

"To midnight services, if it's any of your business," Corinne said, regal as a queen. Just like always.

"Now Walter this wasn't my idea..." Shipwreck started to say.

"Yes it was too," Corinne said. "You know I wouldn't ever ask anyone to go to a church they don't belong to. But you said you hadn't been to a real Episcopal midnight service since before the war, and you'd be happy to drive us if that was the only way we could get there tonight."

"Why you need a cabbie in a sailor suit to take you to church on Christmas Eve?" My head was spinning. I heard another siren off in the distance and my gut clenched. I was running out of time.

"We need somebody to take us because of you, Walter," she said flatly. That set me back.

"What? Because of me? Why?"

"Daddy won't take me and Mama anywhere, not even church, because we couldn't make you quit pestering us. So Shipwreck is going to drive us, and he ain't even going to charge us, either. Me and him have been talking about church and the meaning of Christmas every night now for a while."

I looked at Shipwreck. "Every night?"

"I drive her home from Dawson's," he said. "I got night shift all the time now."

"So I heard."

Shipwreck had a pretty good idea what I had in my pocket. But he tried to talk like he wasn't afraid, like this was just a conversation. From all those combat ribbons I saw on his blouse before he buttoned his bridge coat, he had a lot of practice pretending not to be afraid. Enough practice to dive into a bottle when the war was over and never come out. I didn't like him being afraid of me, but there was nothing I could do about it.

"So I was pestering you," I said to Corinne.

"You know what I mean," she said. "You should have let things settle down, Walter."

"I just drive her home, Walter," Shipwreck said. "For God's sake, I'm old enough to be her daddy. I drive her home and we talk about stuff."

"Like the meaning of Christmas," I said.

"That ain't none of your business," Corinne told me. "That's none of your business now, Walter."

"It never was any of my business," I said.

"It almost was." Her voice turned so soft I almost couldn't hear above the wind and rain. I stepped a little closer. "It could have been your business," she said.

"No," I said. "I've never tried to mind anybody's business but my own." I was really close to her now.

She wrinkled her nose. "Walter, you smell like a French whorehouse. And you've been drinking, too. Not beer either!"

I couldn't believe she used the very same words Shattuck had used about the smell of the spilled perfume. But that was silly. It's what everybody said when someone was doused in perfume. I wondered if all that expensive perfume would soak into the pavement in front of her house and rot in the sun and begin to stink like the fish guts did after Bull went fishing.

"It was your Christmas present," I said. "A bottle of Chanel Number 5. The best. Not something cheap. I tried to take it by your house tonight." My voice caught, but I had to tell her what was waiting for her when she got home. Maybe that was why I had come over here in the first place. I couldn't keep my thoughts straight. "Your father knocked me down and tried to stomp me. The perfume broke."

"Is Mr. Valland dead?" Shipwreck said. He sounded amazed at the thought that maybe the blood on my shirt was Bull's.

"Why would Daddy be dead?" Corinne looked at him like he was crazy. "It's a miracle that the only thing of Walter's that got broke was my perfume." She looked off across the slashing rain. "Chanel Number 5, huh? Pretty fancy, Walter." She almost smiled. Then she turned back to face me. "That was crazy to just go up there to the house like that."

"I guess you're right," I said. "Your mother had to sap

him with a loaded sock to stop him from killing me."

"Oh, Lord!" She thought about that for what seemed like a long minute. "I don't guess she hit him hard enough to kill him, did she?"

"No, he was coming to when I left."

"Well," she said, "there goes Christmas midnight services, Arthur. Mama won't go now 'cause she sinned by whacking him. She'll have to nurse him back to health and feel all guilty about hitting him before she's ready for church again. He'll act like a big baby until he gets over being dizzy. Then it's really going to be hell Columbia around there for a while. I better go home and face the music." She made a face. "I wish she had killed him."

"Let's don't talk anymore about killing anybody else on Christmas Eve," Shipwreck said.

"What do you mean, anybody else?"

"I'll drive you home, Corinne." Then he looked at me. "Is that okay with you?"

"Why ask me?" I said, before she could say anything. Because I knew she would.

I stepped back into the rain to let them go by. Corinne opened a little maroon umbrella and tipped it against the wind to keep the rain off that little hat and her hair

"I'm sorry Daddy broke your present for me, Walter," she said. 'Once he gets over being dizzy, he'll have to go off somewhere and sulk until he gets his pride back. He was going to go fishing down at Cape Canaveral for a couple weeks anyway. You could call me next week and maybe he'll be gone. Dawson's is going to be closed."

"I think maybe I got other plans," I said.

"Oh, well. Okay, if you got other plans." I could tell that she thought I was snubbing her.

"Oh hell, Corinne," I said. "I don't have other plans I wouldn't break for you. But somebody else probably has other plans for me that I won't be able to get out of. I really wish I could call you next week."

"Well call me, then."

"Hell, I wish I could. We might have had some good times once in a while if we ever got the chance."

"We had some good times already," she said, and smiled at me.

I stood there with my hands in my pockets, still hiding the gun, and she couldn't see my tears because of the rain running down my face.

"Go on," I said. "Go home with Shipwreck. You're getting wet. That lousy no-good son-of-a-bitch!"

"You're way wetter than I am." She almost smiled again. "But you really ought to stop calling my daddy that. Only I get to call him that, but not even me on Christmas Eve."

"I'm not talking about your daddy," I said. "I'm talking about somebody else entirely. Two somebody elses." I looked over at Shipwreck. "Just take her home, will you?"

"You done 'em both?" Shipwreck finally asked.

"Both of 'em," I said.

"Jesus. Was I number three?"

"I don't know, Shipwreck. Sorry, Arthur. I don't think so."

He seemed to let a big breath out that he had been holding, and nodded.

"What are y'all talking about now?" Corinne said. Her little umbrella was fluttering in the wind like it might collapse any minute.

"What we're talking about will keep," I told her. "Go on, get out of the rain will you?"

"You might as well tell me what you're talking about. You know I'll find out soon enough."

"That'll be plenty of time then," I said. "Soon enough is plenty of time."

"Okay, smarty-pants." She turned away.

"I do wish your daddy hadn't broken your present," I said to her back. "Chanel Number 5 is supposed to be the good stuff."

She half-turned back and almost lost the umbrella. "It isn't the gift, but the giving we share, for the gift without the giver is bare."

"Get out of here with your lousy Georgia folklore," I said. "Go home before your nice outfit is ruined." I was pretty sure that in the rain that neither one of them could tell that I was crying.

"The saying means that giving the gift is what counts, not how expensive it is," she said, walking away. "Or whether it got broke. Nobody can ever break it that you tried to give me a nice Christmas present, Walter."

What could you say to that? The hard cold rain washed the sting of my tears away. When I could see again, they were getting in the cab. I walked down to the street with my hands still in my pockets. The wind suddenly came so hard I had to sidestep to keep my balance. I realized that I was drenched and shivering hard. Sally's Christmas tie was soaking wet and whipping over my shoulder on the wind. I wondered suddenly if any of Shattuck's blood had got on the tie. That would be the final straw somehow. I couldn't bear to look just then.

Shipwreck started the cab and Corinne rolled down the passenger window. "Call me after Christmas," she said above the wind. She never turned loose of an idea once she had it.

"If I can." I had to raise my voice to be heard. I moved closer. "Okay, I'll call you if I can."

"You call me," she said. "To hell with Daddy. We'll think of something."

"Goodbye, Corinne," I said.

I watched the tail lights out of sight, shivering badly now in the cold rain. Then something big and four-legged, and black as a bad dream, came gliding from behind a wind-tossed hedge of Spanish bayonet and growled at me like Godzilla.

"Just leave it in your pocket, Walter," Billy called out, somewhere behind me in the blowing dark. "We might as well do this easy. I don't want to have to roust out no doctor to treat a dog bite on Christmas Eve."

I took my hand off the gun it in my pocket, and Billy came up behind me and took it away from me. When he stepped around beside his dog where I could see him, he was pointing a lever-action Winchester carbine one-handed, with his thumb on the hammer, just like John Wayne in the Westerns.

"What the hell's the deer rifle for?" I said.

"Some people go off the deep end when they get in a shooting scrape, Walter." Billy's big Western hat was flapping its wings like it wanted to fly, but he had it snugged down with a chin strap.

"What's that mean?" I said.

"The first kill's always the hardest, just ask me," Billy said. "After you get that first one out of your system, some people seem to get a tail wind up, and just keep on shooting people."

"Jesus Christ, Billy! You think I was going to shoot Corinne?"

He leaned his rifle back across his shoulder and scratched behind his Dane's ears. "Maybe Shipwreck, since those assholes told you he was beating your time with her," he said "I knew you'd be here as soon as Jerry told me what Shattuck said tonight about Shipwreck. I was afraid you might be started in on a real front-page Christmas massacre."

I just shook my head.

"You never know with shootings." Billy waggled the butt of his carbine. "Jerry told me you had what looked like a .45. A .30-30 trumps a .45 any season of the year."

"You're something else, Billy," I said. "You really ought to be in movies."

"Yeah, yeah, and I guess you really ought to be in jail, Walter. That's where I have to put people who shoot people, even pieces of crud like them two."

"Okay," I said. "Let's go."

"With any luck they probably won't be too hard on you, Walter. Two against one, two known assholes and bullies against a nice guy. Who knows? You'll probably only get a manslaughter rap. Maybe a little vacation down to Raiford will do you good. You been looking run down lately."

"Jesus Christ, Billy, you've got an awful sense of humor." I was shaking so bad now that my teeth were chattering

"It helps out in an awful world," Billy said. "Let's go on in now, Walter. I got hot coffee over at the lockup."

"Okay," I said. "Let's go on in. It's cold as biddy be damn out here."

Jacksonville Beach, 1993 (continued)

I cannot tell you how I wish your mother would have lived long enough for those miracle drugs to finally cure her of TB. She died the year they made the announcement that TB was almost entirely done away with in the United States. Of course they were wrong, like they're wrong about so many things. But a lot of people got well on those drugs. It seems like she finally just got too worn out to go on living. I hate to think it had anything to do with what happened to me.

Nobody I talk to now has any idea how scared everybody was back in those days about things like TB and polio. I was quarantined in Orlando once, because of an outbreak of polio. It seemed like you could almost smell the disease in the air. You could for sure smell the panic of everybody who was trapped in town. People did some wild things to get by the roadblocks. I flagged down a through Greyhound from Tampa to Atlanta and bribed the driver forty bucks not to tell the cops he had stopped for anybody. It was money well spent even though the cops never asked him.

People will always be afraid of something. While I was in jail it was nuclear war and the Commies. Now it's AIDS that I hear a lot about everybody being afraid of. It will always be something. Maybe even TB again, before all is said and done. Or somebody worse than the Commies or the Nazis will come along. People will always be terrified of something. I have learned that much in this lifetime.

I know your mom's parents were the only real parents you ever had for most of your life. I know they raised you good. Maybe you wonder why I never wrote to you after I went away or tried to come and see you after I got out. Maybe you're just glad I didn't. I figured you'd be glad for me not to have anything to do with you, because you stopped sending me Christmas cards after you got out of high school. I figured your grandmother made you send Christmas cards before then whether you wanted to or not. Your grandmother was real big on Christmas and birthdays, stuff like that. I figured after you grew up and moved out and she couldn't keep after you about sending me a card, you probably just moved on with your life. I didn't know what else to think. And that was really the right thing for you to do, just get on with your life.

I did drive through the town where you are living now. I mean now when I am writing this, not when you are reading it of course. I rented the dishwasher's pickup truck for the weekend. I had started wondering how you looked now (now that I am writing this) grown and married and with kids of your own. That was quite an adventure all by itself, because I hadn't been behind the wheel of a car since they impounded my Chevy the night Billy arrested me. I guess it's like a bicycle. You never forget completely. I made it to your town all right. But when I got there I was suddenly afraid to even drive down your street to get a glimpse of you or the grandkids. I guess I went into kind of a panic because that's how I got in the trouble I did, hanging around trying to get a glimpse of somebody else's life from the outside. I heard on TV that they call what I did back then "stalking" (I wrote it down). They seem to have a word for everything nowadays, but that sounds awful.

I don't even know how to write to you as a grown woman without getting all mixed up in my mind about how you looked in your cute little dresses your grandparents picked out for you, how you always wanted to unlock the Chev when we went places, or that time we saw the cows chase that deer--even that doll I got you that last Christmas. It's still hard for me to imagine that you're

238

a grown woman and a mother now. I don't even know my grandchildren's names and probably never will. I don't mean to make you feel bad by saying that. It's just the way it is.

I don't know if you told husband or children anything about me. If you don't want them to know anything about me, I've tried to keep it that way. I asked the lawyer to be careful to talk only to you when the time comes, so as not to spill the beans to your husband. He said he would be careful. It's the best I can do at this late date. I guess I just hate the thought of everything that you know about me being what they put in the newspapers back then. Or worse, what they wrote in those true crime magazines.

The newspaper stories came from the trial and the testimony, some of which was bad enough. Those true crime magazines just made up whatever they thought would sell magazines. I was a real desperado by the time they got through with me. I wonder if you ever read that newspaper feature story that said I wore the same necktie every day of my whole trial. I don't know why that was news, but the tie was the one you gave me that last Christmas. Billy had it dry-cleaned for me out of his own pocket to go with the only suit I had left after my other one got tore up that night. I wore that necktie the day I got out, too.

Like I said, the prosecutor wanted to make an example of me. I wouldn't take the deal he offered me to tell him about the *bolita* operation, so he was going to fix me for that, let alone the shootings. I think he saw the shootings as his shoehorn into the numbers racket, and then when I wouldn't play he really got mad.

Maybe you think I was dumb to keep my mouth shut. But those people were the closest thing to friends I had, all the way from Mr. T. down. Mr. T. got me work in North Florida after the hotel in St. Pete fired me, remember. He said he felt an obligation. Ronnie and Donlevy closed up the apartment on the Beaches. Donlevy sold my Chev, and sent the money to your grandparents for you and Chris. Your grandmother wrote a nice note to me to say the money helped out a lot.

From what she said, it was an awful lot of money for a used car and some old furniture. I've always thought Ronnie chipped in some of his own, too, or maybe it came from Mr. T. Donlevy came to see me in jail and told me they'd handle all those details and not to worry about anything. He said he told your grandparents to call him if they ever got in a bind. I don't' know if they ever did, because I lost touch with Donlevy after I went to Raiford. He and Ronnie were allergic to prisons, you might say, and never visited.

Never once did any of the *bolita* people threaten me about talking to the prosecutor, though he seemed to think they must have. It just wasn't like that. They knew me better than that. I always minded my own business and no one else's, and they knew that.

There was one thing funny that happened in the trial. Funny hah-hah, not funny strange. At least I thought it was funny. The prosecutor was bound and determined to drag Corinne through the mud and prove we had a hot and heavy affair. I guess he thought that would help make the first-degree murder charges stick. He had copies of the motel register that I signed in St. Augustine. I told him I was by myself. He knew better, but he couldn't prove it.

So he subpoenaed Corinne as a witness and told me that he was going to break her on the stand and smear her good if I didn't cave in and do the deal. He didn't know anything at all about her if he thought he was going to get the best of her, so I just kept saying I was by myself. But he was cocky as hell. He was holding her back until the last minute, trying to pressure me. The press was all there the day she was supposed to testify, all set for the juicy details he had promised them.

That day Bull Valland walked into the courtroom. He was wearing an old-fashioned dark-blue double-breasted suit and carrying a white Panama hat. He looked like a Sicilian in a movie, not a retired Georgia fireman. He sat down right in the front row, right up behind the State's Attorney's table.

He didn't look at me the whole time. He just stared a hole through the prosecutor. You could feel the weight of that stare all the way across the room. Billy was sitting at the prosecutor's table when he looked around and saw Bull. I saw him nod and I saw Bull nod back – maybe a half an inch – without any change of expression at all. I don't know what Billy said, of course, but I know Bull had some kind of Cracker clout in Southern politics and even Billy was leery of him. Maybe he was a Grand Kleagle or some damn thing

Billy leaned over and told the prosecutor something. . The prosecutor spun around like he was going to stare Bull Valland down. He couldn't do it, and the whole courtroom saw him not be able to do it. He turned back around and hunched his neck in his shoulders and damned if he didn't look afraid. I almost felt sorry for him then. But he should have known better than to try to mess with Bull Valland's daughter.

The prosecutor put off calling Corinne all day long. He wasn't nearly as smooth as he had been up until then. He kept clearing his throat. And he couldn't help himself – he kept sneaking glances back at Bull. Bull never moved, never looked to right or left. I wondered if anyone else in the courtroom could feel the tension. Billy looked like he wished he was someplace else. The press was getting restless, waiting for the red meat.

At the end of the day the prosecutor announced that

the prosecution rested, without even calling Corinne. The judge had to gavel down the sudden outbreak of surprised voices from the gallery. Corinne walked out of the courtroom with that flat Indian look on her face that made her look like her daddy. She had been prepared to do battle all right. She was probably mad at Bull for not letting her get into it with that prissy prosecutor.

I never saw her or her daddy again. My lawyer told me I had to testify if I wanted to go for self-defense, and stand up to the cross-examination. It was pretty rough all right. The prosecutor tried to take it out on me for all the face he had lost by not putting Corinne on. He hammered at me for two whole days on the stand.

He had a snowball's chance in hell of getting me to say anything about Corinne as part of any romantic triangle. He actually tried to get a rise out of me by saying she was dating that asshole Shattuck. My lawyer objected to that as not in evidence and he came back with well I must have thought she was, or why shoot him?

I just kept repeating that I was jumped by those two for no good reason and shot to protect my life, over and over. He tried to make a big deal about me having a gun in the car, like I was planning something, but having a gun in your car was legal in Florida back then, and I think he lost some jury support right there.

They weren't willing to go as far as self-defense, but they stuck to second-degree murder. My lawyer said it was because I fired a second shot after I had both of them down. I was surprised, in a way, how relieved I was that I didn't get the death penalty; I pretty much felt my life was over anyway and whatever happened next was just details.

To this day, though, it tickles me, how Bull Valland walked into that courtroom and just owned it, without saying a word. He protected his daughter in the end, so he was all right in my book.

State prison wasn't really all that bad. A couple of the wardens who came and went through there over the years knew all about Dawson's Famous Seafood Restaurant, and I wound up as more or less the head cook down there for a long time. When they started hiring people to staff the kitchen, I still did most of the work while they sat on their asses and "supervised." The state paid me pocket change for it, too. Handling the big portions wasn't all that different from an Army mess hall or a big retirement hotel, and the planning kept my mind occupied.

I had tons of time to sit in my cell and read and I went through the entire library, pretty much. I never had any trouble with the tough cons, because I came in with the rep as a shooter with mob connections. That was one reason – the other was why mess with the cook, who can fix you for keeps on the chow line without anyone the wiser. It wasn't the life I would have chosen, but it's the life I had.

Don't worry because I wrote stuff about *bolita* and all that, or the things I said about anybody. Almost everybody who might object is dead, even Bull Valland. I am amazed that the state of Florida runs the lottery now, not the old outfit. But I guess you know that. Corinne and her parents moved back to Georgia long before I got out of jail, according to the only people left on the Beaches that I knew. They said she took a job as a hospital dietician, if you can believe that. I bet she gave those doctors and nurses something to remember, too. I didn't try to get in touch with her. I didn't see any point in bothering her again. There was just too much water under the bridge.

Please believe I always loved your mom. How I felt about Corinne had nothing to do with that. It's beyond me to explain, but it was a whole separate thing. I was kind of crazy about her that year, but my whole life had turned kind of crazy, with your mother sick and you gone.

Corinne was really something. Regardless of all that happened, I don't regret the time I spent with her for one minute. I don't ask you to try to forgive or understand any of this, and I'm sorry if saying that about Corinne hurts your feelings. But you are my last living kin (plus your children, of course – though it feels funny saying my grandkids) and you deserve to know.

Love, Walter (your dad)

Thank you for reading.
Please review this book. Reviews help others find
Absolutely Amazing eBooks and inspire us
to keep providing these marvelous tales.
If you would like to be put on our email list to receive
updates on new releases, contests, and promotions, please
go to AbsolutelyAmazingEbooks.com and sign up.

Bonus

By going to The New Atlantian Library website (NewAtlantianLibrary.com) and entering the password below into the Bonus Reward Section, you can read a another short story by William R. Burkett, Jr. – for **free!**

AA1026

About the Author

William R. Burkett, Jr. published his first novel at 18. He was a strapping youth who lived with his grandparents at Neptune Beach, Florida. His first job was as a copy boy for the *Florida Times-Union* and *Jacksonville Journal*, but that soon gave way to a position as feature writer. After a tour of duty as an M.P. in Germany, he resumed his journalistic career. While working in both the States and the Bahamas, he pursued a particular muse – duck hunting. That led to writing for hunting magazines and doing PR for the Washington State Highway Patrol and settlement in the Pacific Northwest where the ducks were plentiful and the fishing was good. Although he cut his teeth as a science fiction writer, this novel proves he has a good sense of drama and a serious turn of phrase.

The New
Atlantian Library

NewAtlantianLibrary.com
or AbsolutelyAmazingEbooks.com
or AA-eBooks.com